NIGHTSCRIPT

VOLUME ONE

EDITED BY C.M. Muller

CHTHONIC MATTER | St. Paul, Minnesota

NIGHTSCRIPT: *Volume One*

FIRST EDITION

Cover: "Nøkken" (1904) by Theodor Kittelsen

Additional proofreading by Chris Mashak

Nightscript is published annually, during grand October.

CHTHONIC MATTER | St. Paul, Minnesota
www.chthonicmatter.wordpress.com

CONTENTS

Everything That's Underneath | *Kristi DeMeester* | 1

Strays | *Gregory L. Norris* | 11

In His Grandmother's Coat | *Charles Wilkinson* | 20

The Cuckoo Girls | *Patricia Lillie* | 32

The Sound That the World Makes | *David Surface* | 44

Below the Falls | *Daniel Mills* | 57

The Keep | *Kirsty Logan* | 68

She Rose From the Water | *Kyle Yadlosky* | 72

Animalhouse | *Clint Smith* | 78

Tooth, Tongue, and Claw | *Damien Angelica Walters* | 100

Momma | *Eric J. Guignard* | 111

The Trees Are Tall Here | *Marc E. Fitch* | 123

A Quiet Axe | *Michael Kelly* | 131

The Death of Yatagarasu | *Bethany W. Pope* | 133

The Cooing | *John Claude Smith* | 137

A Knife in My Drawer | *Zdravka Evtimova* | 143

On Balance | *Jason A. Wyckoff* | 149

Learning Not to Smile | *Ralph Robert Moore* | 159

Fisher and Lure | *Christopher Burke* | 180

The Death of Socrates | *Michael Wehunt* | 186

A Preface to Darkness

———◆———

"I delight in what I fear." SHIRLEY JACKSON

Welcome to the inaugural offering of an anthology which aims to sate your appetite for strange and darksome tales. As a reader, I am irresistibly drawn to this sort of fiction—fiction which, in the hands of a specialist such as the one quoted above, implants its weird seed into the reader's mind and thereafter blooms into something so very satisfying to behold; something which, in the days to come, we cannot avert our attention from. Stories with resonance. But I suppose that's the ambition of any fiction.

Nightscript, then, exists in part to showcase a select few of the numerous talented scribes currently operating in the field of literary horror—or whichever appellation you choose to affix to this type of fiction. And while the twenty tales collected herein certainly wear that categorization well, there are reasons to delight in each which go far beyond their gray to midnight gradations. These are carefully-crafted works told in a variety of styles, and containing, perhaps most importantly, a powerful emotional core.

It is my hope that this anthology series will continue to find its way into your hands for many an October to come, and that you will join me for that invigorating walk through the darkness. Let us delight in what we fear.

C.M. MULLER

EVERYTHING THAT'S UNDERNEATH

Kristi DeMeester

———◆———

CARIN LEFT THE door ajar for Benjamin. He'd come inside only once that day smelling of sawdust and ice and swallowed the sandwich she'd made for him, pecked her on the cheek, and returned to his project. When he went, cold air swirled through the kitchen and caught at her hair and cheeks, and she stilled her hands which reached to grasp the shoulders of his coat.

"A door," he'd told her.

"We have a door."

"No. Something solid. Something good," he'd said.

The next week he'd rented a saw, borrowed a truck from Tom next door, and dragged home a pile of lumber. At night, the smell of cedar leaked inside of her, and she dreamed of great trees, tangles of limbs and roots reaching deep into the earth under a blood red sky. Redwoods and Oaks and Cedars wrapping tight around her body, squeezing until she fought for breath. Her ribs and sternum cracking under the impossible weight.

"I don't like the smell," she'd told him that morning, watching the liquid movements of his body as he pulled on his thermals and boots. Every movement calculated and precise. She'd fallen in love with him while watching those delicate hands fold and unfold a napkin.

When was the last time he'd danced? She couldn't remember.

Even that was a lie. Of all the things she'd learned to believe these past three months, this was the easiest.

"Everyone likes the smell. It keeps moths away."

"I guess I don't."

"It won't be as strong once it's done. You won't even notice it."

"Sure."

"Don't come out okay? I want it to be a surprise."

For hours that day, she'd stood at the kitchen window, her hand against the glass, listening to the sharp bite of metal against wood. The sound of her husband slowly, carefully putting it together again.

Something solid. Something good.

Outside, full dark had fallen, and still the saw whined.

Surely a door was a fairly simple thing? Benjamin was no carpenter, but he'd watched videos online, read articles, and it seemed easy enough. A Saturday project. Something he could finish in one day, maybe two if he ran into any snags or really screwed something up.

He'd hidden himself behind the large shed in their backyard. When the realtor had shown them the house, Benjamin had turned to her and smiled, slow and quiet. The secret smile he kept just for her. His lips mouthing the word "studio." They'd put an offer on the house that afternoon. He'd just started the renovations when his vision began to blur and his toes had started to tingle and go numb.

Now and then she would see the top of his hat or a sudden dervish of sawdust caught in the air, but she never actually saw *him*. She tried not to worry. The doctors had said his prognosis was good, that he should be able to carry on as normal with a few slight modifications. That she shouldn't feel the need to hover over him, waiting and watching for another day like the one where she'd found him on the floor of the shed, shaking and whispering that he couldn't feel his legs.

After four doctors, two specialists, and six months, they'd finally received a diagnosis. A pink-lipped, blonde doctor, her voice light and giggling like a young girl's, telling him that he would never dance again, that M.S. would slowly take away everything he had ever known. Ever loved. How Carin had wanted to slap that baby-voiced, Barbie-faced bitch and tell her to talk like an adult instead of a goddamn child. Her palms had itched with the want.

Again, she went to the kitchen window and looked for him in the gloom.

He hadn't turned on any lights. She frowned. He did this sometimes. When he was immersed in a rehearsal or in new choreography, he would forget to eat or to sleep. Once, when they'd first been married, he hadn't come home, lost himself in the tying together of music and muscle, and she'd spent the night curled in the bathtub, the water turning cold around her. The next morning he'd hugged her to him, his chest and stomach hard under the dark sweater he wore, and swore that he would love her until his body couldn't remember how to breathe.

Still. He shouldn't be using a saw in the dark, and she moved toward the door that led into their backyard.

She called his name into the black, the wind whipping her words away from her before the winter night swallowed them. Shivering, she stood in the doorway taking her right foot on and off of the top stair. The saw came to life for a brief moment before settling once more into silence.

He's fine. He can take care of himself. He's not a child, she thought, and she turned back, left the door slightly open for him. He would be disappointed if she went to him and spoiled the thing he'd worked on all day. Especially now. As if the disease blooming inside of him had already eaten through what little he had left. As if she didn't trust him to be able to do this thing for her. Something so simple. A thing a husband should be able to do for a wife.

With methodical care she cooked a dinner she wouldn't eat and packed it in the refrigerator in case Benjamin was hungry when he finally came inside. There was a decent bottle of Malbec, and she opened it, didn't bother with a glass.

At midnight, she was drunk. Somewhere beyond the kitchen, Benjamin hammered at the door, and the rhythmic pounding coupled with the wine made her sleepy. Leaning into the couch, she closed her eyes and vanished into the smell of clean wood. Somehow, it had seeped into the house, stealing in through the crack at the bottom of the door. It didn't bother her anymore. Benjamin had been right.

It could have been hours or minutes later when the sound woke her. A light scritching, like something wrapped in heavy fabric dragging itself across the hardwoods. She caught her breath and willed her heart to be silent and listened to the heavy silence of the house. One. Two. Took a breath and let it out. Slowly, slowly. Tried not to think of the fear curling hard and sharp in her belly.

The sound stopped, and she had the distinct feeling of it moving, turning back. Something crawling on its belly from the kitchen toward the back door.

Benjamin must have come inside because all of the lights were off. He would have gone through the rooms and switched them off one by one, moving quietly to avoid waking her. She could picture him stumbling in, tired and aching from a long day of work, and letting the door fall shut behind him without the latch catching properly before going to bed. An animal—a squirrel or a possum—had found its way into the house seeking warmth from the frigid night. This was the sound. Had to be the sound she heard now. She couldn't let herself think of the possibility of anything else.

The sound had turned, was moving away from the kitchen door. The crawling thing making its way out of the kitchen, past the dining table on the left and toward the living room where she lay trying not to breathe. Whatever the animal was, it was much larger than she had originally thought. A dog, maybe? But why would it creep around like that, dragging itself along on its belly?

She could hear its breath now, slow and even. Certainly not a squirrel or a possum. Too large for that. Too large even for a dog. Something the size of a man. Benjamin had not closed the door, and now an intruder had slipped between their walls, would open her up with his teeth and use the parts he could. This was what she thought as she listened.

Her heart hammered in the back of her throat, and she squeezed her eyes shut, willed herself to move, to scream, to do anything but keep still. It was a simple thing to sit up, to reach over and switch on the lamp resting on the end table next to the couch, but the thought of the creature on the floor kept her frozen in place.

"Carin?"

Her breath whooshed out, her lungs burning and aching.

"Benjamin?"

"Are you awake?"

"What the fuck? Are you okay? What are you doing?" She sat up quickly, reached a hand for him, but he shrank away from her, tucked himself further into darkness. She squinted but could only make out the outline of his frame prostrate against the floor.

"Come to bed with me."

"Did you fall? Let me help you."

"Didn't fall. Just worn out. Didn't want to wake you. Come to bed with me," he said again. His voice was strange. Tired. Like he used to sound after a long day in the studio.

It didn't explain why he'd been crawling in the dark.

He must have fallen. He would have been ashamed, wouldn't have wanted her to know that it was happening so quickly. The disintegration of this graceful body. His own private hell laid bare.

"Yeah. Of course," she said, stood, and without thinking, reached for him again.

"Carin? Who are you talking to?" The voice, Benjamin's voice, came from directly behind her. Not the form lying before her in the soft dark. Her knees buckled, and she stumbled forward, the room suddenly flooded with light as Benjamin turned on a lamp.

There was nothing there. No strange man huddled in the corner, no terrifying doppelganger of her husband. Only the paisley area rug and a large basket she used for laundry next to the fireplace.

Turning, she looked at her husband. Rumpled t-shirt, his hair tousled from sleep.

"I was dreaming," she said, but even as the words left her mouth she felt the untruth in them. They fell from her tongue like dead things.

"You were talking," he said and smiled.

"Overly tired. I do that sometimes."

He nodded and pulled her to him. His skin smelled of cedar, bright and clean, but as she breathed, the smell turned sour, almost fetid, and she pulled away.

"Come to bed," he said and reached across her to turn off the lamp before moving down the hallway. For several moments, she waited, let her eyes re-adjust to the darkness and listened to the mattress springs creaking beneath Benjamin's weight. She would not look back into that corner. She would not.

When she made her way to their bedroom, Benjamin was already asleep. That night, she locked their bedroom door. Outside, the creature moved up and down the hallway. She did not sleep.

"I'm thinking of carving it. Making it more intricate. Interesting. You know?" Benjamin took a bite of pancakes, smiled at her across the table.

"What?"

"You sick or something?" He reached for her face, brushed her bangs away from her eyes. A gesture he'd made habit while they were dating, but it had been so long since he'd touched her like this. Something light and affectionate not tainted by the darker thing lurking under his skin.

"No. Didn't sleep well," she said, and he nodded, tucked back into the stack of pancakes before him.

"Your appetite."

"Mmm?"

"You haven't been hungry like this. Not for a while."

"I guess so."

She pushed her fork into the cooling stack of pancakes on her own plate, pulled it back and watched as the holes filled with syrup and closed over like blood clotting a wound. When he'd woken that morning, stumbled into the bathroom, she went to the door, thought of whispering through the wood about the sound, that *thing* creeping up and down their hallway, but she swallowed the words, laughed at how stupid she was acting. She was stressed. Hadn't slept well in months. There had been no sound. No second Benjamin.

"I didn't know you could carve," she said.

"Something about the wood. It's hard to explain," he said. She looked at him, but he kept his eyes down, focused on the plate before him. Whatever had come in the night may have been a product of her mind, but she could still hear that soft scraping, could still hear the sound of a body pulling itself up and down the hallway.

"Don't come out okay? I want it to be a surprise."

The repeated phrase bothered her. She set down her fork.

"I've never seen you carve," she said, and he glanced up at her then. Blue eyes cold and burning, and she immediately regretted intruding on this moment. He wanted to impress her. To show her that he wasn't beaten yet, and here she was doing her best to fuck it all up.

"Of course. I'll be here. Getting drunk. Maybe wandering around naked. You'll be missing a good opportunity."

He grinned at her, his eyes flashing, but then snatched up his hat, kissed her, and whispered in her ear, his breath sweet and cloying.

"There's so much we can't see. Everything that's underneath. Hiding. But it wants us to see, to pull it out from where it's sleeping and make it beautiful again."

He was out the door before she could open her mouth.

SHE STOOD IN the hallway flicking the overhead light on and off. Ten hours. Benjamin had been outside for ten hours. There was the dim thought nibbling at the back of her mind that she should be worried, that he could have collapsed again, but right now, there was only this. In that moment between light and dark, vague, amorphous shapes coalescing, rising and falling like breath. If she flipped the switch as quickly as possible, she could almost make out hair.

How long had she been standing in the hallway? Benjamin's words were still in her ear, swelling and bloating with impossible weight.

"Everything that's underneath," she repeated.

She'd come looking for some evidence, some sign to prove she wasn't crazy. A groove carved into the floor, a hair, anything that justified the reality of the sound she'd heard in the night. Pulling herself onto her belly, she crawled along the floor, her cheek pressed against the wooden boards, fingers probing.

After an hour of doing little more than bruising her ribs from crawling along the floor, she gave up. It was when she turned out the light, in that brief flash, that she saw something. Each time she thought she saw more of the shape, but then she doubted herself. As soon as the light was on, she absolutely believed that it was nothing more than her eyes playing tricks, and so she flipped the switch off again, squinted into the growing dark.

The back door opened and closed, but she did not turn away, did not look back over her shoulder to see her husband creeping through the kitchen, his fingernails digging into the floor. Surely, he would be creeping. All of the things slumbering inside of him coming awake, waiting to be seen, waiting to be found in the dark.

"Come and see, Carin," he said, and she flicked the light once more. On. Off. The shape did not move, but she could make out what looked like teeth. She thought she would laugh, or cry, or scream, but every sound stayed locked in her throat.

"Come and see the door. Come and see what I've found," he said.

"I can't. Please," she said. If she followed him now, the world would come undone. All of the shadows would come to life and grow teeth. Bite and tear until there was nothing left.

"It's so beautiful, love. Come and see."

"Please, Benjamin," she said, but somehow, her legs carried her forward. Her fear, hard and razor sharp, unfolded inside of her.

He waited for her on the back steps, his legs scrabbling across the wood like a spider's, and led her out into the night.

It had begun to snow, but the flakes looked tinged with grey, as if night had stained their surface, and she swiped at her hair, afraid that somehow by simply touching it, the darkness would leak, like poison, into her as well.

She followed him past the row of Camellias she had planted, past the vegetable boxes she had put to bed back in October. Her feet were freezing. She had forgotten to put on shoes.

There was no light in the shed, but she could hear him before her, that slow, methodical dragging.

"Benjamin?"

"Can you see it? The whole world opened up. Waiting." His voice was high, breathy with excitement.

It took a moment for her eyes to adjust, to take in the massive cedar door Benjamin had built. He'd suspended it somehow—a series of ropes and pulleys—and it hovered above the ground. Strange wormlike shapes with round mouths and jagged teeth carved into the surface, their bodies tangling together in some kind of obscene orgiastic experience. Here and there a proboscis extended, probing into the chests of what appeared to be human torsos, the hands held up in supplication.

"So beautiful once you open the door and look. Once you *really* look. Like the wood. Waiting to be seen and touched. Then it opens you up, swallows down all of the sin and the hurt and the damage. You can't imagine. What it's like to be whole again."

He stood then, his full height towering over her, his toes cracking as he extended his body into arabesque, laughing as he went en pointe. Something his body should not be able to do.

Behind her came the sound of something pulling itself on hands and knees through snow.

The door really was beautiful. Deep amber tints that glowed without light. A color she could wrap herself in and forget this past year. All of the struggle and pain and doubt that she'd had in herself and her marriage. Wondering if she was truly strong enough to carry Benjamin—to carry the both of them—through a future that promised only loss.

"Don't you want to open the door, Carin?" Benjamin said, and turned, his pirouette a quick, almost violent movement.

Benjamin's lips did not move, but his voice came from behind her. A voice that belonged to deep earth and snow and dark. A gaping mouth waiting to take everything that had left her bleeding and raw.

"Something good," she whispered.

Benjamin laughed, his body turning impossibly fast, moving into a blurred fouetté. She had forgotten how to breathe. The smell of Cedar everywhere.

Then, she laughed, too, and opened the door.

Strays

Gregory L. Norris

---•---

A BABY SOBS somewhere in the murk beyond the few hundred square feet of your new prison, a studio apartment in a tall house with dark shingles perched on a hill whose back faces the city's downtown. Lately, you have trouble telling dawn from dusk, because the days have all bled together, the one before no different than the next to follow, the summer indistinguishable from this new autumn. A baby crying, its plaintive mewls in sharp contrast to all other sounds like cars on streets and the neighbor's television, which blares through the layers of ancient horsehair plaster from God-knows-when, fake wood paneling put over it in the Seventies, and cheap paint slapped on in the decades since. You wish somebody would attend to that baby's needs. Help the poor thing. Shut it the hell up.

You track its howls. It's down there in the weedy patch of dirt that passes for a parking lot for those residents who have cars. A ghost on four legs, black, darts into the scraggle of diseased trees. Soon after, the baby screams—likely having encountered this other stray orphan. You steal a deep hit off your cigarette, gag on the noxious taste, your stomach curdling. A flick over the rail of the set of rickety steps leading up to the apartment's door sends the embers of the still-lit cancer stick onto the parking lot of the next apartment house, situated below yours. There's a jack-o'-lantern in one of the windows, its features backlit by a flickering candle lodged where living heads have throats. Its eyes stare at you without blinking. Its jagged smile mocks your unhappiness.

You came out for a smoke, and to see the bats that roost under the Route 125 Bridge. The bats fly every night around sunset. They sail and slither through the sky by the hundreds if not thousands. Thousands of bats. They're not here. It must be morning instead of twilight.

Another baby cries from somewhere in your new neighbor-hood. Turning back toward your prison, you're sure there are more stray cats living here than bats. You've never seen so many homeless, hungry animals, and your flesh crawls as that sound again rises, sharp and painful on the ears, greeting another day.

FOUR HUNDRED SQUARE feet, maybe. The studio space is divided by a half-wall that grants an illusion of separate living room space. But on the other side of the partition, the bed is only a few short paces away from the kitchen sink, stove, and a shitty refrigerator that chugs all night and barely keeps the milk cold. At least the narrow closet of your bathroom has a door.

Smoking is a new vice for you, more fallout from the divorce, the foreclosure. You don't smoke inside the apartment. Still, the stench of full ashtrays from tenants past permeates the place. All of the sorrows from untold souls forced to exist in the back apartment of the brooding old manor house at 11 Park Street in Haverhill, Massachusetts have seeped into the walls. You are surrounded by anger and tears, by ashes. Whenever you gaze out your four windows or down the back stairs, a legion of stray cats is visible darting over sidewalks and side yards. Close your eyes, and their sad, insane yowls chase you.

Face it, you're a stray now, too, just like the cats. And face one other truth you haven't wanted to acknowledge since the rainy afternoon you lugged the last of all you owned up those stairs, into this hopeless hovel: the place is haunted by more than the sad cries of stray cats and cigarettes smoked by former tenants.

AUTUMN HUMIDITY LAYS rotten over the city in October, so you sleep with your windows open. There's no air conditioning; you'd use it if there was, despite the last of your money going to the month's rent. You don't know how you'll pay the electric bill, let alone November's rent when it comes due on the first, which creeps ever closer.

Sleep hasn't been easy, your nights fraught with worries about utility bills, the roof over your head—as cursed as this place is, it's all you've got—and food. The fridge grumbles and groans. You've hit up two food pantries within walking distance and have plenty of peanut butter and white rice, but little else. Poverty, however, isn't what denies you sleep on this stagnant night. Movement, from somewhere close by, teases your ears and gossips across your sweating flesh in icy ripples. Not quite footsteps.

Your eyes shoot open. On your spine with two pillows funched behind your head, you face the window beside the front door. The misty orange glow from the streetlamp in the lot of the nearby apartment house oozes into your tiny living space, a view screen of sorts, presently blank. Eyes wide, breathing no longer easy or even involuntary, you wait. But not for long.

A shadow cuts across the window from the inside of the apartment. You bolt upright, a moan dying on your tongue. It sounds even to your ears like a terrified child's as you reach for the lamp, switch it on, sure there's somebody in here with you.

The lamp sprays bald light on the sad landscape of cardboard boxes and other relics that have survived the detonations and dust clouds of your failed marriage. There's no one there. You're all alone. At least you pray that you are.

ON A MEMORABLE gray morning in the blurry succession of days after you move in, you hear noises coming down the side of the half-wall facing your bed, what sounds like a breeze riffling through sheets of paper. Given your inability to sleep of late, even this might as well be cymbals crashing together or a gun's report. You stir, your bleary eyes tracking the sound and, at first, you sell yourself on the lie that you're still asleep, dreaming what you see. The pattern of electric-blue circles on the horror's spine undulates as it skitters down the wall, threatening to hypnotize you. The fast-moving coordination of its multitude of legs paralyzes you to the spot and unleashes revulsion deep in your guts, perhaps born of some primitive race memory.

It skitters closer to the bed, and your horror doubles at the very idea of the enormous black centipede with the bright blue circles working into the bunched bedclothes at your feet, touching your skin.

Going on instinct, you jump up, ball your hand into a fist, and pound the centipede as it performs a truncated figure eight. You draw back; see the foul, inky stain blooming over the wall, which weeps nicotine whenever you boil water on the stovetop. The horror has disintegrated except for a chorus line of tiny dismembered legs twitching and flexing in uncoordinated jerks.

More of its dismembered limbs wiggle against the back of your hand, affixed to your skin by a smear of poisonous purple color. You wash your hands, wash them again, stopping only to retch into the toilet.

NOTHING ABOUT LIVING here is easy.

You don't own a car anymore, so to shop for groceries—with the little money dwindling in your wallet—you walk down the hill, sure you're going to stumble and then tumble along the sidewalk, all the way to the bottom of the world. The worst follows in reverse: walking back up that hill, your arms laden with shopping bags. If the drop doesn't kill you one way, your heart's going to explode in your chest on the upswing.

Doing laundry? The same. There's a coin-operated mismatched

washer and dryer in the basement, but the one time you used them, your clothes came out stinking of other people's sweat. There's a Laundromat in the plaza near the grocery store. Getting there comes with the same financial and travel risks as shopping for food, so you're wearing your clothes longer than you normally would, airing them out, washing them in the sink though that really doesn't cut it in the humidity. That, and the days have gotten shorter, so there's less sun to help with the drying. They'll be colder soon, too.

There's another reason you don't go in the basement. Since landing here a broken man, an orphan with no friends or family, you've repeatedly questioned whether or not you're losing your wits. You sense eyes upon you, telegraphed in gooseflesh and odd startles at night; in moving shadows glimpsed from the corner of the eye and the dark emotions that rise from the pit of your stomach whenever you hear the crying-baby wails that curse this forsaken corner of the globe.

Losing your mind, you avoid the basement because you believe the vast, dark house on Park Street is haunted. There's a *wrongness* down there, you're sure.

ALL DAY WHEN you should be out looking for a job you instead pace, holding the crumpled pay-up-or-quit notice from the slumlord in your clenched hand. The nightmare of missing the rent takes a backseat to a building, abstract fear that has yet to identify itself. You walk the floor, your body's primitive registers warning of the approaching storm.

At night, violent thunder sweeps through. You sit in a huddle, hands covering your ears to drown the cannonade. And then the power goes out.

When you are able to will your legs out of their paralysis, you see the city beyond sitting dark except for candles and emergency lights. The jack-o'-lantern is still there, grinning at you a full week after Halloween. In the deathly silence between thunderclaps, your heart gallops. Alone in the dark, you feel the wrongness in this place intimately. Rain spills down, hammering the house. An angry wind howls around the eaves. The language of the eviction notice plays out again, projected onto the screen of your mind's eye. Where the hell are you going to find five hundred bucks in the time specified? You have a few dollars for cigarettes. When was the last time you ate?

You imagine being homeless on this night, out there in the storm, like the hundreds of stray cats that inhabit the shadows and the neighborhood's unhappy spaces. You, huddled in a dark corner, your belly aching, your muscles tense, mind driven to madness by lack of sleep and an abundance of terror.

The storm throws itself at the apartment house. You sit in the dark, rocking back and forth, drift deeper into your thoughts and, eventually, a state that's not quite sleep.

IN THE MORNING, the neighbor's television blasts through the wall, drawing you out of your fugue. The power's back on, but not in your apartment. You check switches. The fridge that barely runs when the juice flows sits inert and silent, and exudes a musty odor when you open the door to confirm the truth. A circuit breaker's been tripped. The electrical boxes are down in the basement. You resume pacing back and forth across the patch of threadbare blue carpet that always stains the bottoms of your socks a greasy gray.

There's a bite in the air that wasn't present before the thunder rolled in. It works the chill already inside you deeper, into your molars, your marrow. You find the old flashlight you used to keep in the car among the contents of a cardboard box full of your past life's puzzle pieces. It still works. You exit the apartment, tromp down the outside stairs, and round the building. The storm has chipped away at the house's exterior, damage in evidence in the numerous shakes scattered across the parking lot.

You enter the front hallway, where the mail is delivered to a row of metal slots. The space smells stale, gritty. Dirt tracked in crunches under your soles. Water stands in stagnant, shallow puddles. You pass the mailboxes and the soaring staircase to the left, the last trace of grandeur from when this house belonged to one of the mill barons who made his fortune, you've been told, off the sweat of the common people. From somewhere up the staircase, you hear your neighbor's television. A white fluorescent circle illuminates the top of the basement stairs. The smell of other people's dirty laundry hits your nose a few steps down.

The laundry area stews under more cold white bulbs. What few windows exist are narrow and oblong, the glass covered in chicken wire to prevent burglars from breaking into the place. The washer chugs. The dryer turns. So does your stomach. That giant centipede originated down here, you're sure. You switch on the flashlight and force your legs forward into the dark space beyond the laundry area. An arch leads to the gas meters, which hiss and tick. You shine the flashlight. Its beam illuminates the electrical boxes, their corresponding apartment numbers identified in black magic marker on curling strips of masking tape. You locate yours, flip the main breaker left and then right. Done, you turn to leave.

A low whisper drifts from the dark realm beyond, where there are no windows. Your body reacts with gooseflesh and a chill that tumbles down your spine. You shake it off, pivot, flash the light. The back part of the cellar hides behind an old door with flaking paint and a rusted knob with filigree details. That door was closed, you swear, when you first entered this section of the basement. Now it sits partially open, the source of the breeze.

No, get out of here, a voice in your thoughts urges. *Don't go in there!*

You shine the flashlight across the door's scabrous surface. Just one look at what's back there tempts you. You're going crazy after all, you think, punctuating the statement with a humorless chuckle. You push on the door with the flashlight. It resists, as if—

There's somebody on the other side, pushing back...

But then the door cooperates, croaks open, seeming to welcome you into the windowless tomb beyond. You're struck by the smell of sour earth. The beam drops to a dirt floor, crisscrossed in spots by patches of white mold. The beam falters—you muse that the darkness behind the door is so concentrated that it erodes light, like a black hole in deepest outer space. Somewhere, a cat shrieks. A chill shoots through your blood. A stray cat has gotten into the house and is trapped in the basement. Maybe even in this very room. The sound echoes, terrible to hear. The flashlight ticks; its light wanes. Almost lost to your ears is the soft groan of the door, only now it comes from a place that doesn't match the mental map you've drawn of your surroundings. Behind you? When did you enter the room?

You jiggle the flashlight. The beam surges back, revealing the only other landmark in the room apart from brick walls and infected earth. A staircase, nowhere near as elaborate as the one in the front hallway, soars up from the dirt, runs the length of the bricks, goes nowhere. The cat's disembodied sobs power up.

You shuffle backward, your heels kicking up dust. The door, if it closes…

A creak sounds, not behind you but out in front. Another follows, and more after that. Footsteps, coming down the staircase that leads nowhere. You aim the light. The beam flickers. Right before it goes out completely, it scatters shadows across the bricks in the shape of a body. Footsteps, moving closer, closer.

Your back reaches the door, now almost closed. You drop the flashlight, turn, and pull on the cold, rusty knob. The door resists, preventing escape. Someone is coming down those stairs!

You focus all of your willpower into the effort, vowing to tear the door off its hinges if you must. The door flies open, and you run.

Run through the basement and up the stairs, out the front hallway, and back to your prison with its paltry few hundred square feet of room and its scoping view of the downtown.

IN THAT OTHER life and time before Park Street, you read about or saw a documentary on the domestication of felines; how it's theorized that cats, at some point, learned to mimic human baby cries as a way to garner our sympathy.

For days—or it could be longer, because the modern calendar no longer matters—you've heard the cat moving around behind the walls. More than a hundred years have passed since this manor was carved up, its layout redesigned with horsehair plaster and then cheap paneling. Hell, there could be a dumbwaiter behind that wall, whole passageways sealed up, certainly room enough for a stray cat to get lost and trapped.

It mewls, sobs. That sad human baby cry gets into your head, knocks around the inside of your skull. You pace, not eating, only smoking. You'll smoke until the last coffin nail is gone. Then, when you're evicted and living *out there*, you'll raid the public ashtrays, even pick the remains of butts off the dirty sidewalk, wrap your lips around filters already smoked by other mouths and suck down the dregs like you've seen some of the homeless do on your rare ventures downtown.

The cat trapped behind the walls howls. It sounds near, really close now. Behind your walls—*yours*, until the sheriff shows up and removes you from the premises. Maybe it got into the basement, skipped up those sinister stairs in the darkness in its search for escape, found a gap in the bricks, a dumbwaiter or secret passage to nowhere. You wonder how many other doomed souls are lost inside these walls.

You track the mewls, the sobs, to the bathroom. The stray cat's back there, behind the paneling. If you peel open a corner, you might free it. The wall behind the sink. The mirror.

A shimmer of movement draws your eyes up to your reflection, and terror results at the image gazing back. In the mirror is the face of a feral creature, a stray, surrounded by walls that have absorbed decades of ash and suffering.

You open your mouth, and the sound that emerges is crazy with fear, that of a scared, sobbing child.

In His Grandmother's Coat

Charles Wilkinson

————— ◆ —————

WHEN THERE WAS still no sign of him by nine o'clock, and not a creak on the floorboards above, Angela went up the narrow wooden staircase to her son's bedroom and knocked on the door. He was at the age when boys become insistent on their territorial rights. There was no sound, not even a barely audible, blanket-muffled groan or the surf-like sigh of someone rolling over. She pushed down on the handle and peered in. The white triangle of a turned-back sheet was visible in the half-light; then with a shock she registered the dark shape at the foot of his bed.

"Wyll?" she said, even though it was far too small to be human. She could make out a small head attached to a long body with a sinuous snake of a tail. For a second, she considered calling her husband, who was coppicing somewhere in the grounds.

But it would not do to make a fool of herself again. Could it be an otter? That hardly seemed likely, even though they lived near a river. At least it wasn't moving, slithering towards her across the floor. With great caution, she stepped into the room and, hugging the wall, edged her way round to the nearest window and drew the curtains. On the floor was a pair of his trousers, the black ones he wore on schooldays; they had rucked up at the waist line, the curl of the belt trailing behind. She gave a chug of exasperation, picked them up and draped them haphazardly over a chair. Most women had teenagers who lolled around the house for hours, but Wyll must have crept out at dawn. Otherwise she would have heard him moving about.

She stooped down to rescue an abandoned blazer and shirt. A pile of text books was under a table rather than on top of it. Admittedly it wasn't an easy room to keep tidy. No one had got round to attaching purpose-built shelves to the uneven half-timbered walls, and the floor sloped so dramatically that there was only one place where a chest of drawers had a chance of staying upright.

Given the chance to view it, she would never have consented to live in such a house.

WYLL WENT INTO his grandmother's room and took off all of his clothes. So far it had been a good Saturday. He had avoided speaking to his mother by getting up very early and then spending the morning in the forest. At last he had found the courage to dispense with the footpaths and follow the course of the river until he came to a spot where it would be possible to swim naked when the weather warmed up. By the time he returned, the car and the truck were no longer in the drive. Although it was irritating to discover his mother had tidied his room, he decided that nothing would deflect him from his purpose.

He had never met his grandmother, but her room, which his parents had not got round to redecorating, reflected the tastes of an older generation. The Victorian samplers in gilt frames and stiff still lives of fruit and flowers held no appeal for him, but he liked the full-length mirror, which was freestanding and could be wheeled away from the wall so as to reflect a better grade of light. He inspected himself, starting with the auburn hair that his classmates at his primary school in the city had so disliked, along with his brown freckled nose and sharp green eyes. In contrast to the color in his face, his body was luminously white; his limbs well-proportioned but not muscular. Since his move to the country, he was stronger and healthier. Yet there was something vulnerable about his body, as if it had only just hatched in the cold Welsh winter: an animal without a pelt or a shell. He needed protecting.

A month ago, he had discovered the writing beneath the carpet. It was not in any language he recognized, certainly not English, French or Welsh. It was carved rather than scratched onto the black polish of the uneven floorboards beneath the loose carpet in the farthest corner of the room. As it was carefully lineated, he suspected it was a poem of some sort, perhaps in the form of a blessing, a prayer or a curse.

He went over to the wardrobe, took out his grandmother's mink coat and put it on. The satin lining was agreeably cool on his shoulders and back. Beneath the scent of moth balls was a hint of French cigarette smoke and gin. He returned to the mirror. The reddish brown fur reached his ankles and, like his hair, had the colors of fallen leaves darkened by rain. Light rippled across the coat as he wriggled his arms down sleeves that were far too long for him. She must have been a very tall woman; he crouched down for a moment, hiding himself in the coat.

His grandmother had spent most of the middle of her life abroad. He imagined one beautifully shaped leg in high heels protruding from the half-open door of a low slung sports car. But towards the end of her days she spent most of the year in Wales. Wyll wondered if she was watching from the shadows as he stood up, still wrapped in the coat's opulent warmth. Her ashes were in the pale blue Wedgewood urn on the mantelpiece.

He walked over to the corner and lifted up the edge of the carpet. Ever since he had taken to wearing the coat of the woman who must have written the poem, he believed himself to be on the brink of understanding, not the whole work, but the first lines at least. Clothed in the fur she had once touched, he would come to understand the message left for him.

THE UNWASHED PLATES in the sink suggested her son had returned for lunch. Yet there was no sign of him, even though his English tutor was now seated at the kitchen table with a mug of tea. In spite of her plentiful apologies, she was not sorry to have the tutor, elegant in a blue jacket and well-cut trousers, to herself. His shoes, polished to a metropolitan gleam, contrasted favorably with the prevailing culture of trainers and muddy wellingtons. And he had a dark, princely appeal quite at odds with his profession. A classicist by training, he helped the special needs department at her son's comprehensive, a source of income he supplemented with private English tuition. She could hear her husband angrily chopping wood at the end of the garden

"Of course, some of the traits you mention, the forgetfulness, the chronic lack of punctuality, are common indicators of learning difficulties, but there's no chance of getting him statemented. He's really very bright. His vocabulary is excellent. It's simply his spelling and presentation that let him down."

"Well, I'm so sorry, Mr. Brampton, that you've been put to all this trouble. I really feel I should offer you some…" She got up and walked towards her handbag.

"Please no, I insist. Any losses I have incurred are more than compensated by your hospitality"—he waved in the direction of the remaining teacake—"and excellent company. And it's Miles, please."

"Are you quite sure? I feel terrible," she said, holding her leather purse, "I would have reminded him, but he was out so early this morning…"

"Please don't worry about it. What I'd really like to hear is that you're feeling better…in yourself. They did tell us what happened."

She put the purse back in her bag and turned on the hot water tap in the sink. "Well of course, one never really gets over something like that," she said quickly, with her back to him. "But I've had some…professional help. It's been beneficial, I think."

"Good. I'm glad to hear it."

"I just wish we weren't so isolated. Sometimes I hear strange sounds in the forest. And occasionally you catch a glimpse of them, moving very quickly at the water's edge."

"Sorry?" he said, as he picked up a dish cloth and moved alongside her.

"The creatures."

"What kind of creatures?"

"Mink. You probably haven't lived here long enough to know that Wyll's grandmother, who was very far from being the chapel-going kind of Welshwoman, ran a mink farm just a mile or two away from here. Local gossip has it that she was cross-breeding the American mink with something…" Her hands were still in the reassuringly warm water, but she had stopped washing up.

"You were about to say?"

"Something…older. Complete nonsense, of course. It's true the breeders did experiment. The coats of mink kept in captivity are different to those that live in the wild. I'm afraid Wyll's grandmother was by all accounts a rather unpleasant woman, and so it suited the locals to make up stories about her. What is certain is that when she lost interest in the farm most of the mink were freed by an animal rights group…or just let loose. Nobody is quite sure which…"

"I'm surprised the environment people…"

"You mustn't do the drying up. Otherwise I will insist on paying you."

He looked at his watch: "I should make tracks, I'm afraid. Or I'll be late for my next pupil."

They walked down the dark corridor and out onto the drive. It was dusk. And so for a moment Angela did not realize it was her own son who was on the front lawn. The blue-brown mass of the forest at twilight towered above him.

"Wyll," she said, once he was crunching across the gravel towards them. "You do realize you've missed the lesson Mr. Brampton very kindly came here to give you?"

The boy did not reply. With the light behind him, Angela found it hard to read the expression on his face.

"Never mind," said Miles, taking several paces towards Wyll. "Next time I hope I'll have a double delight: the company of both of you."

It appeared Wyll was about to reply when Miles stepped forward, his right hand held out as if to pat the boy companionably on his head or shoulder. Wyll shrank back at once, putting himself well out of reach.

"Oh," said Miles, "*Noli me tangere.*"

"What does that mean?"

"It's a pity you haven't had a classical education," Miles replied, his arm still held out as if he had been frozen in the act of signaling a boundary. "But then practically nobody has these days. 'Don't touch me.' That's what it means."

"I do think you owe Mr. Brampton an apology, Wyll." Her husband was still hammering away somewhere in the undergrowth.

At the very moment Wyll crossed his arms, Mr. Brampton let out a shriek and flapped his hand wildly.

"What...what's the matter?" Angela cried.

"I've been bitten," he said, taking the handkerchief out of the top pocket of his jacket and staunching the flow of blood. "It must have been a horse fly or something, I suppose."

They looked around. Not a gnat was in flight.

"It does look quite deep," continued Mr. Brampton, dabbing at the wound with a handkerchief. "I think I'd better get back and put something on it. Quite a nip in the air this evening," he added with an effortful smile.

As Mr. Brampton walked towards his car, Angela looked in the direction of her son. The treetops behind him were touched with western fire. She remembered how in the months after his birth, when they insisted she must be reunited with him, she held him in her arms—and then noticed the first auburn curls on his head. "Where on earth did you spring from?" she'd said.

THE DOCTORS WARNED his mother not to have another child, but she took no notice. Then it died and she redoubled her interest in him. And so Wyll was forced to take long walks to avoid her grief and organizational prowess. There was also the business of the extra tuition. After it had been discovered he had the mildest form of dyslexia known to mankind, she decided to pay Brampton to give him extra lessons, which was absurd when one considered the school would have provided them for free if he had needed them.

The forest was quite dense now, although he could still catch glimpses of a limpid blue sky through the branches. Beneath the canopy the light was soft brown, turning to dark green where the foliage was at its thickest. He'd been walking for about half an hour when he came to a fork in the path. The path on the left, which was little more than track, sloped downhill and was narrower. He had a good idea where the right-hand path came out. Well today was a day for getting comprehensively lost, he thought, as he broke into a trot and plunged down under the dark arch of overhanging branches. He had only been going for about five minutes when he emerged on a bridle-path that ran beside the banks of the river.

He recognized the spot at once. There was a bend where the river was wider and deeper, its flow more sluggish. It was one of the places he had found for skinny dipping. The path was seldom used and he could always hear the voices of walkers or the hoofs of the horses in time to dive into the black shadows beneath a nearby stone bridge.

But then one day a man emerged from the track through the forest. Wyll had just waded out of the river and was still some distance from his towel. The man looked at him appraisingly for a moment before making his way along the bridle-path and over the bridge. As Wyll dressed hurriedly, he remembered he had seen him somewhere before, but it wasn't until the next day, as he was walking towards the main school building, that he remembered where.

"Who's that man?" he'd asked a boy who was about to overtake him on the way to the foyer.

"Go away, Wyll. You're a notifiable disease."

"Is he a teacher?"

"Sort of...special needs," said the boy, before rushing on.

Further research revealed that the intruder was Mr. Brampton. When they inevitably passed each other in one of the long echoing corridors, Mr. Brampton merely nodded and said "Aha, the solitary bather."

Wyll crossed the bridge. The countryside was sparsely wooded now. There was a stile at the end of the track and beyond an open field in which stood a wire fence that was surrounded by some low wooden buildings with pitched roofs. Although arranged in rows like the makeshift army barracks of the Second World War, they were too small to have served a military purpose. As he drew closer, Wyll realized the place could only be his grandmother's abandoned mink farm. He stepped through a hole in the fence. The nearest building had exposed rafters and the door was missing. Wyll peered through. The metal cages, streaky with gold-brown rust, were still in place. Three or four of the mink would have been kept in there together. Apparently it took about forty of them to make a coat. His mother had told him that the poor creatures were gassed before being stripped of their fur. Nevertheless, it had been a profitable business for a time.

As he walked back in the direction of the bridge, he recalled the animals were permitted to live for about seven months. Seven merciful months longer than his baby brother, born without drawing a proper breath. He wondered if the mink knew what was happening to them. Could they smell the gas? Or hear the death-whisper as the taps were turned on?

When he had tried to put an arm round his mother, as he felt sure he should do, she pushed him away, without turning or looking in his direction.

MILES BRAMPTON WAS half an hour early for his lesson with Wyll and so there was time for a cup of tea in the kitchen. She warmed the pot and took three biscuits out of the tin.

"Is that drawing one of your husband's?"

He was pointing at a picture of the house. The artist's use of broad charcoal strokes captured the building's jumbled timbering, skewed chimney stacks, oddly angled leaded windows—and the great black front door, which was not centrally placed, but appeared to have been inserted as an afterthought into the left wing of the building.

"No, I don't think so. We had it in the living room of our flat. I didn't appreciate it was a picture of a real house until we came to live here. I thought it was some Welsh expressionist's nightmare or an illustration for the Mabinogion."

"Did you ever meet the old lady?"

"No, my husband didn't get on with her."

"But she left him the house."

"Not exactly. Wyll inherits it when he's twenty-one."

Vigorous sawing was succeeded by the sound of timber being split by an axe. She glanced out of the window, but there was no sign of her husband. Although the noise appeared to have come from comparatively close by, it was plain that he was working in the woods.

"I've some news. But I'm not quite sure how you're going to feel about this."

She looked at him narrowly. He had been visiting them for several months. More recently he had taken to turning up even when no lesson was arranged for Wyll. The spring term would begin in another week.

"I've been offered a job at a school in the Midlands. One of the few with a Classics department."

"Oh."

"I'll take it if you...and Wyll...come with me."

"Well, that's..."

A chainsaw started up and then rose to a shrill scream, as if her husband was signaling an intention to deal violently with the wood.

"Please...I can tell you don't like this place."

"You must understand I can't leave...while he is still here."

"I said Wyll can come too. I know he's not exactly fond of me. But he'll find more to do when he's closer to the city."

"That's not the point," she said, turning in the direction of the window. The chainsaw stopped. Nothing stirred on the lawn or the path leading to the back door. The treetops moved very slightly in the breeze. "I think I'd better go and find Wyll. He was in earlier, but it would be just like him to forget again."

Without looking in Miles's direction, she left the kitchen. Now she came to think of it, she hadn't heard Wyll moving around upstairs. Perhaps he had gone out already. She went quickly up the narrow stairs, but stopped as soon as she reached the landing. She listened. There was a faint sound above her, like a fingernail scratching wood. No doubt it was simply a tiny creature alive in the flying beam. She put her head to Wyll's door. Silence. As she straightened up, she asked herself why she hadn't knocked. She wasn't her normal self; something was askew. Was there a straight line in the house? The timbering appeared almost…tangled. She knew the carpenters used wood that had been deliberately bent out of shape, like the cruck beam in the end gable, but as she looked around her everything was subtly deformed: the corridor twisting from her, as if it were trying to hide an additional room in the house. As quietly as possible, she moved away from Wyll's door. For months now she had sensed he was up to something in his grandmother's room. She inched forward until she was standing right outside the other door. Just as she was about to turn the handle, she drew back. Sweat broke out on her forehead; a ribbon of cold perspiration tickled her spine. She stood very still and tried to control her breathing.

Wyll was in his bedroom. Alone in the house. At least that was what they thought. It had not been easy persuading them that, at sixteen years of age, he was capable of spending a few nights at home without his mother. The doctor and the social worker both imagined he must be in a state of shock. Well, they were mistaken. He wasn't even slightly surprised. Once a closer look was taken at his mother's medical records, they would realize that what had happened was all too foreseeable.

Mr. Brampton's kind offer to stay over had been especially unwelcome, but fortunately the social worker was not enthusiastic about it either. And now they were gone and he was lying in his bed, flat on his back, with his arms dangling outside the sheets. He had left the curtain slightly open so he could just see the sharp points of stars in front of the snow-skid of galaxies. The house was quiet. Although spring had almost come, the nights were cold. Moonlight patched the bottom of his eiderdown with silver.

He stretched out his hand, so as to stroke the soft fur of a creature on guard below the headboard. There were four of them altogether, one positioned on the floor at each corner of his bed, and reassuring to the touch. Whilst they were predominantly invisible, it was possible to catch a glimpse of them, usually by coming into the room unexpectedly, or by turning on the light in the small hours. If one was facing you, you would see white teeth flaring and the blaze of red-brown eyes. And then the creature would be replaced by something quite ordinary.

How long would his mother be away this time? The birth of his brother brought back her depression; his death had deranged her. Wyll could sense her insanity without hugging her, which she wouldn't allow in any case. Inside her was a black flame feeding on dark wax. If he stretched out his hands, he could feel the heat of her mad grief pushing him away. And his father hadn't coped either. Instead of trying to comfort her, he'd immersed himself in the estate and, in less than a week, chopped enough wood to last them seven winters. Then there'd been the accident with the chainsaw.

After the double funeral, which she'd refused to attend, Wyll managed to get medical assistance for her. The school had helped.

It was unfortunate that just when she was making a partial recovery, she should disturb him, kneeling, hunched and full-coated in the corner, even his head and feet fully covered by the pelt.

What was important now was that tomorrow he would examine the writing under the carpet without interruption.

He knew there was the weave of every week, its sometimes colorful patterns: the reassurance of the well-stitched routine. And then beneath this lay the secret script: the truth outside the self. It was his task to decipher it and find how it matched the text of his dreams. Then he would know who he was and what he would become.

AND AS FOR her husband, just because *they* thought he was dead…

At her with their bone-dry doctrines, they were; but she knew how flesh formed in the wind and an invisible hand grasped the axe.

As for Gwyll! The name chosen by his grandmother, the price of the legacy that rescued them from poverty in the city, didn't they know what it meant? No matter how often you called him Will, he was Gwyll, a thing sent to creep at dawn and dusk. Why should she put her arms around him, let him suck her breast? Almost from the first she had known what he was. They sent him away so he could get his milk.

Did they think she didn't understand that all the creatures his grandmother had bred were in the forest, waiting to enter the house? Of course she did.

She wasn't prepared for what was in the room. At first there was only a stump of fur, but then came the writhing within, and next lumps like small heads bobbing beneath the pelt. She remembered how she thought that if she could bring herself to touch them gently all the agony would stop. But as she took a step forward, she saw a mouth part; an eye opened in the teeming fur. Another one joined it, shiny with terror. And then forty mouths were wide, waiting for the hiss of the gas.

THE CUCKOO GIRLS

Patricia Lillie

———◆———

SHE JUST WANTS to finish her folding in peace, to escape the laundromat's overwhelming smell of bleach and the shrieking toddlers running laps around the tables and carts, but the strange girl appears intent on making Jennifer her new best friend.

The girl looks about seventeen—a hard, worn-out seventeen, but still seventeen. She sounds about twelve, both in voice and conversation. She says she's six weeks pregnant, but her belly looks more like eight months along.

Jennifer is shocked when the girl says she's a dancer at the Wild Cherry. Jennifer's always assumed strippers are about boobs and butts, not bellies and babies.

"It pays good money," the girl says, "and they buy me fast food, so I'm good." She babbles about her boyfriend, her job, and the two extra coats that somehow ended up with her laundry the last time she was here.

"I found them when I got home," she says. "They were really great, even if they were too big. It was like Christmas."

"Somebody probably missed them."

She looks at Jennifer, her eyes wide. "I never thought of that."

Jennifer revises her opinion. The girl looks fifteen. Jennifer finishes folding and packs up her clothes. She double-checks to make sure she has everything. She doesn't want any of her things accidentally ending up in the girl's basket. Her wardrobe is sparse enough.

"I'll help you carry out your stuff," the girl says.

"No need. You probably shouldn't be lifting any more than you have to."

"It's okay. I'm really strong. Dancing's a good workout."

They put the baskets in the backseat of Jennifer's Civic. Jennifer thanks her and leaves.

If the girl ever says her name, Jennifer misses it. It doesn't matter. She doesn't expect to see the girl again.

JENNIFER SITS IN her car outside the laundromat.

Why does she have to be here? The building's plate-glass windows are fogged with condensation, but not enough to hide the girl on the other side.

Shut off the car. Get out. Go in. She turns the key and cuts the motor but doesn't move from her seat.

She's just an irritating little girl.

The girl doesn't bother to sort her laundry. Black, red, white, green, blue—it all goes into one washer. Jennifer is annoyed but doesn't know why. They're not her clothes.

I can leave. She won't even know I was here.

She can't bring herself to turn the key, start the car, and back away. She hesitates too long. The girl sees her. She's out the door and banging on the window of the Civic.

"Hey, Jenn? You need help carrying stuff in?"

She can't remember telling the girl her name.

THE GIRL WATCHES Jennifer put her darks into a washer. "You've got really nice stuff. I'll help!" She grabs Jennifer's basket of whites.

"Thank you, but please don't. I'd rather—" It's too late. Seeing the girl handle her clothes makes Jennifer's skin crawl. *I'll have to come back tomorrow and wash them again.*

They end up sharing a folding table.

"Look! I saw yours and liked it so much I bought one just like it." The girl holds up a purple sweater full of twists and cables.

Jennifer knows the girl didn't buy it. Jennifer knitted the sweater herself, from her own pattern. Well, her own adaptation of a simple pattern. It's one of a kind and customized to fit her.

The girl puts the sweater on. It fits her perfectly.

That's not possible. The girl is tiny, smaller than Jennifer in both height and girth. Other than her belly, which looks slightly smaller than it did when Jennifer met her.

I'm losing my mind. Jennifer tries to remember the last time she wore or even saw the sweater. She can't. She throws the rest of her laundry into her baskets without folding.

"I need to go. I'm running late."

"Bye, Jenn!" The girl's cheerful voice follows her out the door.

THE SHELVES HOLD too many varieties of vitamins and supplements. Their bright labels make Jennifer's eyes burn. There's one for energy, one for vision, one for over fifty, one for under thirty. All she wants is one basic multi-vitamin, but she wants a good one. She's run down and out of sorts. Nothing she can put her finger on, but she hates going to the doctor. Self-diagnosis and a trip to the drugstore are always her first line of defense.

I should have gone to a real drugstore. Talked to the pharmacist.

The super-store seemed like a good idea. *Get everything at once and get home.* Except Jennifer and her cart full of groceries can't make it out of the vitamin aisle. The fluorescent lights give her a headache. She can't make up her mind. The burning in her eyes threatens to give way to tears.

"Hey, Jenn!"

She recognizes the girl's chirpy voice but doesn't turn around.

My little stalker.

"Last night was really busy at the club. Good tips! I get to go shopping today!"

If I ignore her, she'll go away.

"Wow. All you have is food! I'm going to get something orange and sparkly."

Jennifer tries to remember the girl's name. She's sure the girl mentioned it, but she's forgotten.

"Ginkgo biloba is supposed to be good for memory. Ginseng, too."

"How—" Jennifer turns to look at the girl.

She wears Jennifer's purple sweater buttoned tight over her enlarged breasts and distended belly.

It's meant to be a jacket. Jennifer's carefully wrought cables and twists are stretched flat. Her small, even stitches become lattice-work, and the girl's pale flesh shows through the gaping holes.

She's ruining it.

The girl reaches into Jennifer's cart and pulls something out.

"Ohhhh. Raspberry Fudge Ripple! My favorite!"

Lightheaded and dizzy, Jennifer leaves her groceries and the girl in the aisle. She sits in her car shaking and crying for a quarter of an hour before she's able to drive home.

This is stupid. She's just a strange little girl who stole my favorite sweater.

She doesn't know how the raspberry fudge ice cream got in her cart. She hates raspberry, hates it even more when it messes up her chocolate. Raspberry Fudge Ripple is her sister's favorite.

"So, I've got a teenage stalker," Holly says.

Jennifer and her sister talk on the phone once a week. Their parents are gone, and they are the only family left. They may not like each other, but they stick together. As long as that together doesn't involve anything more than short conversations from a hundred and fifty miles apart.

"What's he look like?" Jennifer assumes Holly's stalker is a young man. Holly is always sure any male in her presence is fascinated with her. About half the time, she's correct. Maybe a third of the time.

"It's not a boy! It's a girl." Holly's voice is tinny and empty.

Must be a bad connection. Holly always sounds confident and full of life. Full of herself.

Jennifer wants to tell her sister about the girl. Tell her that she has a stalker of her own, but she knows Holly won't believe her. Holly's the younger sister, but she always does everything bigger and better. At least, Holly thinks so. She definitely does everything louder. If Jennifer tells her sister about the girl, Holly will sneer and call her a copycat. Holly seems convinced Jennifer envies everything about her and wants to be just like her.

If I wanted to be someone else, I'd choose someone I liked.

Holly's still talking. She never waits for Jennifer's answers.

"She's tallish, dishwater blond. A little dumpy. She sort of looks like you at that age. Except she's pregnant. Did I tell you she's pregnant?"

Jennifer realizes whom her girl reminds her of. She looks a lot like Holly at fifteen. Or twelve. Holly blossomed early.

"Mine too," Jennifer says but knows Holly doesn't hear her. When Jennifer speaks, Holly rarely bothers to listen unless they are talking about Holly.

"Gotta run," Holly says. "Date. Maybe he'll protect me from my stalker."

"Next week," Jennifer says, but she's talking to dead space. Holly's hung up.

THE VOMIT SWIRLS and disappears down the toilet. For the third morning in a row, Jennifer throws up. Her period is late. She knows what this should mean, but she also knows it isn't possible.

She's been alone since she stopped seeing Wayne. *Stopped seeing* sums it up. They never exactly broke up.

She watched him sit in her living room, engrossed in a Nature Channel documentary. He blended with the decor. Gray walls, gray curtains, gray furniture, gray Wayne.

"…brood parasites, slyly planting their own eggs in the nests of

others…" Even the voice from the television was gray, drab.

"I wonder if they still make black and white televisions?" she said.

"Are you drunk?"

"Not yet." She took a sip of her white wine.

"…and the cuckoo's oft-targeted host species appear to have developed an instinctual acceptance of the interlopers…"

After he left the next morning, she stopped answering or returning his calls. Eventually, he stopped calling.

A stomach bug. She'd wait it out. No need to visit the drug store. What would she buy? A pregnancy test? *Wayne was six months ago. Or three. Was he before or after the girl?* She thinks before, but isn't sure.

The nausea doesn't go away. She has to pee every hour, on the hour. Her breasts hurt. She stops leaving her house except to go to work. Every time she goes out, something makes her gag. She misses a second period. She's frightened.

"Early detection," says the soothing voice on the television PSA. Jennifer tells herself it's time to put on her big girl panties. She makes an appointment with her doctor.

The morning of the appointment, she finds her purple sweater. It's on the shelf in her closet, right where it belongs. *Was it there yesterday?* She can't remember.

It's not stretched out at all. It fits perfectly. She wears it, for luck.

"Really. I can't be pregnant. It's not possible," Jennifer says.

"We'll do a test anyway," Dr. Yuhaz says. "Just to make sure. How old was your mother when she entered menopause?"

Jennifer doesn't know. She tells the doctor her mother had a hysterectomy after her sister was born and no, she doesn't know why. Nor does she know about her grandmother, who died when Jennifer was six. Her family didn't talk much. Jennifer marked "No" next to Family History of Breast Cancer for years before anyone told her that was what killed her grandmother.

Knowing what killed her grandmother is still more than she knows about her father's family. The only sign he ever had a family is a stack of old photos, all of a single dark-haired man.

"I'll order blood work and an ultrasound, but you are pregnant," the doctor says.

"I don't even have a cat." Jennifer's feet are in the stirrups and she can't see the doctor's reaction, but she hears his laugh.

How would I take care of a child? She puts both hands on her belly and imagines she feels a spark. *I need him.* The ferocity of her reaction surprises her. She's never wanted children. *He's mine.* She is convinced the baby is a boy. *Fetus, not baby. Get a grip.* If she is going to change her mind, she needs to do it soon.

Outside, Jennifer sees the girl across the parking lot. She waves to Jennifer before getting into the backseat of a dark SUV. Her belly is flat.

She must have had her baby.

For the first time, Jennifer wants to talk to her. Ask her questions. It's too late. The girl is gone.

Her cell rings. She doesn't recognize the number, but answers anyway. She feels a need to talk to someone, anyone.

"There's been an accident." The voice on the other end won't give her any details, but Holly is in the hospital.

Holly's stalker. Jennifer looks around the parking lot for the SUV, but it's gone.

"Is my sister okay?"

"She's out of danger, but she's asking for you."

Instead of going home, Jennifer goes to her sister.

It wasn't Holly's stalker, and it wasn't an accident. Holly's current boyfriend beat her up. Jennifer always thinks of Holly's men as The Current Boyfriend or The Last Boyfriend or The One with the Good Job—or No Job or whatever. She rarely meets them and doesn't bother to keep track of their names.

"I thought he'd be happy when I told him I was pregnant," Holly says. "We'd been together eight months!"

Holly's face is swollen to the point of unrecognizable. Jennifer hurts just watching her talk.

"He said he'd had a vasectomy and called me a bitch and a slut."

"You're not a slut," Jennifer says. Holly's a serial dater. She breaks up with The Current Boyfriend as soon as she has The Next Boyfriend lined up.

"The baby's safe," Holly says, "and I'm pressing charges."

"Good."

WHEN HOLLY IS released from the hospital, Jennifer brings her home with her. Jennifer's house is small, but big enough for the two of them.

"Only for a little while. Until I get back on my feet," Holly says. She doesn't have The Next Boyfriend picked out and has no one to help her.

Jennifer takes Holly to Dr. Yuhaz. They both carry boys.

"I'm thinking about naming him Thomas," Jennifer says. Thomas was their father's name.

"No! I'm using Thomas." Holly's lower lip sticks out.

"I claimed it first," Jennifer says.

"I bet I thought of it first."

They bicker, like when they were kids.

Their father hated their squabbling.

"I was only supposed to have one daughter," he said and retreated to his den.

"I'm the oldest so that would be me," Jennifer told her sister.

"Yeah, but if he could pick one, it would be me."

Jennifer never argued about that. Holly was probably right.

"I was Dad's favorite. I should get to name my son after him," Holly says.

"You're right. I give up. I'll come up with another name."

"You can use Thomas as a middle name." Holly is magnanimous. Her pout is replaced by a smug smile.

Jennifer keeps her satisfaction to herself. She never intended to name her son Thomas. He is Bennet, after the man in the photographs.

THE POLICE CALL. The Ex-Boyfriend's crotch rocket is found in a ditch. His body is found about a hundred yards away. There is no need for Holly to appear in court.

Holly works from home and can do her job from anywhere with an Internet connection. *A little while* stretches on.

"I can't bear to go back to that apartment," Holly says. "Bad memories. Bad for the baby."

Jennifer drives the hundred and fifty miles and packs up Holly's clothes and a few miscellaneous belongings. The furniture she leaves for the landlord to deal with.

Holly's neighbor helps load the car. "So. That guy got what was coming to him," he says.

"Yes," Jennifer says.

"Did you hear about his eyes?" the neighbor asks. "I heard they were pecked out by birds. Couldn't have happened to a more deserving guy."

Jennifer doesn't tell Holly.

HOLLY RARELY LEAVES the house. She chatters on her phone and takes over preparing the house for the babies. The room Jennifer calls her office, really a catchall for everything she can't figure out what to do with, is emptied and transformed into a nursery. It's barely big enough for two cribs, but Holly says it'll do for the time being. Jennifer has no input on the decor. When she offers a suggestion, Holly doesn't hear. Her sister is on a mission. *She's nesting.*

On the back wall, Holly paints a forest dominated by a large leafy tree.

"I wanted it to look like a fairytale, but boyish," Holly says. "You know what I mean."

Jennifer doesn't know, but doesn't tell her sister. "Why do the leaves have eyes?"

"They're birds!"

"Oh." Jennifer drops it but avoids looking at the mural. The watchers in the tree make her nervous. They make her think of the girl.

Holly orders everything she needs for the nursery, as well as baby supplies—blankets, onesies, diaper bags—for both of them online, but never answers the door when the deliveries arrive. Jennifer is used to finding packages by the back door.

The latest packages weren't left by the postal service or UPS. On the creased wrapping paper, dancing storks dressed in jackets and hats shout IT'S A BOY! When Jennifer picks up the bundles, one loses its glittery stick-on bow.

"Have you told anybody the name you picked?" Jennifer hands Holly the gift addressed to Thomas.

"All my friends."

Jennifer opens the other gift. The smell of cheap new clothes makes her eyes water and her nose run.

The packages contain matching t-shirts. Holly shakes hers out and holds it up. The orange shirts say *Mommy's Mini Man!* in glittery letters.

Orange and sparkly.

"Ugh. Like I'm going to dress my son in that." Holly tosses the tiny shirt to Jennifer. "You can have them both. They must be from one of your friends."

Jennifer folds both shirts and slips them back inside their wrappings. She keeps the tag that says *Bennet* hidden. She hasn't told anyone, not even Holly, her son's name.

Holly looks around the living room. "You know, we really need to brighten this place up before the boys come."

HOLLY GOES INTO labor first. Jennifer carries her sister's suitcase and is explaining to the nurse that no, she isn't in labor yet—it's her howling sister—when she feels the warm gush between her legs.

"Looks like it's a good thing you're here," the nurse says. She calls somebody to clean up the puddle on the floor.

A nurse delivers Bennet. Dr. Yuhaz is with Holly. Thomas is the older by four minutes, which makes Holly happy. Jennifer lets her crow. She doesn't care who's the eldest.

Filling out the birth certificate, Jennifer writes *Unknown* in the place for the father's name. Which is true. She doesn't know and holding her son, doesn't care. She doesn't ask what Holly writes. *The One with the Crotch Rocket, deceased.*

Both boys are born with shocks of dark hair. The hospital staff can't get over how much they look alike.

"Our father had dark hair," Holly says.

A nurse brings the squalling Bennet to Jennifer's room. "Hush, my beautiful boy," she croons.

Jennifer recognizes the voice. *The girl.* She shakes as she reaches for her son.

"Calm down. He's just hungry." The woman looks like an older, tired version of Holly.

Or the girl.

"You're *my* beautiful boy," Jennifer whispers to her son.

HOLLY AND JENNIFER take the boys to the park. With their matching strollers and identical outfits, people assume the infants are twins and are surprised to find out they're cousins.

"We're sisters," Jennifer says.

"You two must have the same taste in men. Or else there's some real strong genes on your side of the family. But, they really are beautiful babies." The elderly woman's comment is a variation of what the sisters hear every time they take the boys out together. They always take them out together. When separated, the babies scream and work themselves into a frenzy.

"Must be the genes. The first thing we've ever agreed on is the boys," Holly says. It's her stock reply.

Across the park, a heavily pregnant girl sits down next to a woman with a book. The woman's body language tells Jennifer she's annoyed at the interruption.

The girl looks at Jennifer and waves. For a moment, Jennifer thinks the girl is *her* girl. She pulls Bennet's stroller closer.

She's not. Other than their bellies, they don't look at all alike.

"Whatever happened to your stalker?" she asks her sister.

"I don't know. She disappeared around the time I found out

I was pregnant."

"Mine too."

Bennet, or maybe Thomas, lets out a howl, and soon both boys are crying. Distracted, Jennifer forgets about the girls—hers, Holly's, and the one across the park.

The sisters pick up their sons. "Hush, my beautiful boys," they croon in unison.

THE SOUND THAT THE WORLD MAKES

David Surface

———◆———

THEY WERE TOO old for this—that was the thought that kept coming back to her as she watched the bare trees fly past the car window while the hum of the engine blended with Jerry and Gordon's voices and the ancient-sounding croaking of Peter Gabriel coming from the speakers.

"Daddy, are we there yet?" Gordon said in a whiny kid-voice and then chuckled, cracking himself up. Gordon had always been a lightweight since they'd started these midnight rides back in college. One-toke Gordon. At least some things stayed the same.

"Patience, sonny boy," Jerry boomed in his best fatherly baritone, "patience..."

Maddy liked how Jerry still retained some of his actor's skill and presence, even though he no longer used them on stage but in the lecture hall. Jerry had not planned on being an adjunct professor in the psychology department, nor had Maddy planned on being married to one. *Plans change*—that was how Jerry put it. The important thing, he said, was not to be so attached to your plans for the future that you can't handle it when a whole different future arrives.

Jerry's profile against the dim blue light from the driver's-side window could have been the same one captured in the old Polaroid she'd found last week when they were cleaning house. The same proud Roman nose, the same flowing, tousled mane of hair, although occasionally a square of illumination from a street-light outside would pass across his head and show for a moment the balding forehead, the creases and sagging skin around the eyes before the light moved on and darkness covered him again.

"Hey, doc..." She turned and saw Gordon handing the joint toward her. She'd already declined twice, but Gordon, like a goldfish swimming around the bowl, kept coming back to the same spot with no memory of having been there before. Good old Gordon.

Maddy shook her head. "No thanks." They didn't smoke that often anymore, so she knew her refusal would not attract attention. Drinking was a different matter. Jerry had already remarked once about her not sharing their nightly bottle of wine. *You making me drink alone again?* She'd pleaded fatigue and a weak stomach—that much was true. Also, she needed a clear head to finish working on her doctorate. Almost two months since her last drink and her head was anything but clear.

"Jerry," she said, "can you roll down the window, please?"

"It's pretty cold out there, sweetheart," he said.

"I don't care," she said, the harshness in her own voice startling her. Then a little softer, "Please."

Jerry pushed the button, the window next to her moved down a few inches and in a second the cold winter air was all around her, numbing her cheeks and filling her lungs. With every breath, she felt the first traces of nausea subside.

"So how long before we get to this place?" Gordon asked.

"Few more miles," Jerry said with the kind of bold assurance that Maddy knew meant he wasn't exactly sure. "In the meantime, enjoy the pretty lights."

At those words, Maddy suddenly thought of the song that her

mother used to sing years ago when her parents drove her around to look at the Christmas lights. She hadn't thought of it...for how many years? It should have been a good memory, even a comforting one. But the searing pain it caused made her want to tear the sound of her mother's voice out of her head.

"Holy shit," Gordon laughed, "look at *that* one!"

A blaze of light and color appeared on the right and moved toward them. Maddy saw a two-story house strung with blinking lights and a dozen or more illuminated plastic figures planted on the lawn; a nativity scene complete with all three wise men, plus a row of open-mouthed Dickensian Christmas carolers, Santa in his sleigh with all eight reindeer, and even Snoopy smiling blissfully in a Santa hat.

"Jesus, where's the Easter Bunny?" Gordon said.

"He's on his government-mandated fifteen-minute break." Maddy could hear the smirk in Jerry's voice. *Here we are again*, she thought. *Enjoying the things we have contempt for—what would we do without them?*

Maddy felt a surge of nausea returning. *Not now*, she thought, *not here*. Why did she agree to come along on this ride? She was too old for this. Too old and too pregnant.

She'd almost told Jerry about it tonight. She'd planned to, like she'd planned to tell him the night before, and the night before that. But then he'd asked her to come along on this stupid midnight ride out to the country and he'd seemed so excited that she didn't want to spoil it. She was angry at herself now for that. For thinking of him first. That was going to have to stop. That was going to have to stop soon.

Another garishly decorated house rose out of the night and moved toward them on the right. Maddy flinched at the chaos of plastic holiday figures clustered together in the snow.

"Are the giant candy canes actually supposed to be *touching* the Nativity scene?" Gordon asked. "Christ, my parents never spent that much money on Christmas decorations in their whole life. What about your family, Maddy. Did they..." Gordon stopped himself even before Jerry's hand reached across the driver's seat to touch his arm. "Shit, sorry..." Gordon mumbled.

"It's okay, man," Jerry said, patting Gordon on the knee. "Betty and Henry were into all this Yuletide stuff big time. They would have loved all this, right sweetheart?"

Maddy didn't answer. This was Jerry's way of helping her deal with it. No use tiptoeing around or keeping it hidden. Bring it all out, bring *them* out into the open. It was a way of keeping them alive, Jerry said. And it might have worked. If it hadn't been for that item in the newspaper.

It was a single line, a quote from a nameless source, a truck driver who'd seen her parents' car go off the road and over the cliff, who'd *followed the sound of screams to the crash site.* That one line was the worst thing she could imagine, worse, even, than their deaths. It was all she could think about, day and night. She told Jerry and he'd tried to play the therapist with her. That one moment, terrible as it may have been, was not her parents' whole lives. Their lives, he tried to assure her, were more than that, and that one moment could not wipe away all that they were. She listened in silence and thought, *It already has.*

She drank wine and vodka every night to shut off that terrible sound in her brain until the news came from the doctor and she had to stop. No more drinking. No more looking back. Only looking forward to the new life inside her that would be the start of a new life for her too. That was how it was supposed to work, wasn't it? One generation dying to make way for the next? It was natural. But that thought couldn't keep out the feeling that there was still something horrible and unfair about it all.

She glanced up at her own reflection in the passenger window and was instantly sorry. The haggard face, the flesh starting to sag under the eyes and at the jawline. She was going to be forty-one years old in four months. What business did she have giving birth to a child? Who did she think she was? No one ever believes they're as old as they really are. Not even her mother. On one of their last visits, over their third glass of white wine, her mother had admitted that she couldn't believe she was seventy. *I look in the mirror sometimes and I wonder, Who is that old lady?* Old age had taken her by surprise. A reasonable, intelligent woman, she had still somehow thought, against all reason, that it would some-how not happen to *her.* Just as she had probably not thought that she would die in a dark ditch by the side of the road, screaming in the crushed wreck of a car...

Maddy squeezed her eyes shut tight and pressed her fists against them, trying to push the thought out of her brain. When she opened her eyes again, things had changed. It was darker outside the car now. All the lights of town far behind them. They were in what Jerry liked to call *the old, real country.*

Maddy saw a small, ramshackle wood house with several ob-long blobs of ghostly white light standing between the trees. The shapes were vaguely human, with the contour or suggestion of a face, an arm, or a leg, a few smudges of cracked and faded color still hiding in the creases. Maddy wasn't sure if she was looking at a wise man, an angel or an animal.

"Wow. How old do you think those are?" Maddy said. The cold air had made her feel almost normal again. "Guess that's what happens when you can't afford new decorations."

"It's not about that," Jerry said in that all-knowing tone that always annoyed her; tonight it set her nerves on edge. "If those people had a million dollars they still wouldn't throw those things away."

"If they had a million dollars, they would live like fucking trailer trash," Gordon said. Maddy grit her teeth.

"No, no," Jerry said, "that's the *good* stuff. The *real* stuff..."

"You mean it's because they're poor," Maddy said, sounding a little harsher than she meant to. "You think it's cool because they're poor."

No one spoke for a moment. Then Gordon chuckled, "Wow. Someone's grumpy."

"There's nothing *cool* about poverty," Jerry said in his measured teacher's voice. As if she had suggested that there was. "What I love is what they do with what they have. Remember that graveyard in Mexico? Those wooden crosses with the names and dates spelled out in roofing nails and thumbtacks?"

Maddy remembered stumbling through the desert graveyard with Jerry—was it thirty...thirty five years ago? Jesus. She'd agreed to split a hit of acid with him, the first and last time she'd ever done that. The little wooden crosses with their thumbtack names made her think of a child's art project, and before long she became convinced that it was a cemetery for dolls. They'd sat on a stone bench and watched the sun turn the Western sky blood-red, and she'd felt like there was something *in* the sunset, or *behind* it, watching her. It was going to take her with it. She sat there holding her breath longer than she thought was possible, waiting for it to happen, not understanding why it was taking so long.

Jerry was good at seeking out places like that. The strange, out-of-the-way corners of the world. Like the place he was looking for tonight. God only knows where he'd heard about it. This was typical Jerry. *Off the grid* was where the good stuff was, the *real* stuff, and that was where he was taking them tonight.

"Seriously, Jerry," Gordon asked. "How'd you hear about this place?"

"Cosgrove saw it," Jerry said. "About fifteen years ago. He told me about it last year before he retired."

"How come I never heard of it? A hundred and fifty year old monastery is kind of hard to hide, don't ya think?"

"Not if no one's looking for it. They're a separatist group. They left the Church, or the Church kicked them out. Not sure which. It was a long time ago. So they're really off the map."

"So what's this service we're going to see?" Gordon said. "What makes you think they'll even let us in?"

"Cosgrove saw it one Christmas Eve back when he was an adjunct. I asked him how he got them to let him in and he said it was no problem. He said they didn't seem to care if he was there or not."

"Yeah? So what do they do? Sacrifice chickens?"

"No. He just said it was something he'd never forget for the rest of his life. Probably some kind of archaic form of the Christmas vigil." Jerry took a deep breath and started chanting in his best spooky baritone, "*Kyrie...Domine...Dominus...*"

The hills and trees that had crowded around the sides of the road had begun to fall away. Maddy could sense more than see the barren fields stretching out around them. Occasionally the lights from a far away farmhouse would float by in the distance like the lights of a ship far out at sea.

A Christmas Eve Mass. The last time she had been to one was with her parents—how many years ago? She closed her eyes and saw again the glow of candlelight, smelled the scent of pine and hot candle wax. The memory of an old song was stirring inside her chest, almost rising to her throat. What was it? More than once she had awoken with tears on her face from a dream of music so intensely beautiful and moving that she'd thought her heart would burst. Jerry had explained that it was just another trick that her brain was playing on her, that there really was no music, just the sensation of beautiful music that our brains manufacture for us. That didn't seem right to her. Just because she couldn't remember the music, the exact melody or the words, that didn't mean it was never there.

Looking out at the few stars glittering over the barren snowy fields, it came to her—the child she was carrying inside; this would be its first time in church. She decided it would not be the last. It didn't matter what Jerry said about it. It was what her mother and father would have wanted. She would give that gift to her child. And to them.

A light appeared far away in the darkness, a pale glow that looked like a single lamp moving slowly across the frozen fields. "There it is," Jerry said.

Maddy could make out the shape of a rectangular building far off the road, light shining from a single window. Jerry slowed down and turned on to a long, narrow road that took them down into the fields and closer to the building. The road had not been plowed and there were no tire tracks in the snow. The tires rumbled and crunched and occasionally banged over deep holes hidden by the snow.

"Shit," Gordon said, "are we even on the fucking road?"

"Don't worry," Jerry said through gritted teeth as the car banged its way over the rough surface. "We can't get lost. It's right there. All we gotta do is follow the light."

"*Follow the light, Jerry...follow the light!*" Gordon said in a spooky falsetto.

As they drew closer Maddy could see that the building was made of bricks that had once been covered with white paint that had grown thin and worn away. The roof was flat except for a kind of square tower at one end. The windows were all small and dark except for one that threw a narrow trail of pale, weak light on the snow.

"Looks more like a prison," Gordon said.

Maddy looked around and saw there were no other cars or trucks in sight. "Are we the only ones here?" she asked.

"Looks like it," Jerry said. "I guess they don't get a lot of visitors..."

They all sat in the car for a minute, looking up at the tall, weathered brick walls and the single lighted window above. Maddy noticed that Jerry hadn't turned off the ignition.

"Are those *bars* on the windows?" Gordon said. Maddy looked up at what Gordon was seeing, but the small windows were so dark and grimy it was hard to tell.

"Jerry," she asked, "are you sure this is the right place?"

"Absolutely," he said, finally shutting off the ignition. He sat there for another few seconds looking at the building. Then he opened the car door. "Come on."

Maddy's legs sank up to the knees in the snow as they plodded toward the building. "Don't these guys believe in shoveling?" Gordon groaned. "How do they get in and out of this place?"

"Maybe they don't," Jerry said what Maddy had been thinking. No cars, no trucks, no vehicles of any kind. No tracks in the snow, which was four days old by now. Under any other circumstances, Maddy would have concluded that the building was abandoned—if it wasn't for the pale yellow light burning in the little window above. As she looked up, Maddy saw a thin shadow pass behind the window, blotting out the light for a second.

"Jerry," she said, taking his arm. "Look—somebody's home."

"Yeah?" he said with a forced-sounding cheerfulness. "See? I told you this was the right place. Come on..."

They approached a double wooden door set deep into the wall, the old wood painted an ugly institutional brown. "Shouldn't there be a bell or a buzzer or something?" Gordon said.

"Do you think this is the right door?" Maddy asked.

"Hey, do you *see* any other door?" Jerry said, sounding strained for the first time. He reached out, took the doorknob in his hand, pushed, and the door swung open a few inches.

"See?" Jerry said. "If they weren't expecting anybody, why would they leave the door open?"

"Maybe because they *weren't* expecting anybody," Maddy said, angry at the stirrings of fear deep inside her. She had wanted this to be beautiful. She had needed that. She still did. And she didn't want anything or anyone to ruin that. "Come on," she said, stepping in front of Jerry. "We don't want to be late."

The first thing Maddy noticed was how cold and empty it was inside. Bare, whitewashed stucco walls. Worn wood floors. No furniture. No decorations of any kind. Not even any sign that this was a church. "Which way is it?" she whispered. She could see ghost-traces of her breath from the corner of her eye as she spoke.

"Shit, these guys don't believe in turning up the heat, do they?" Gordon said.

"Cosgrove said something about a balcony..." Jerry said. A flight of steep, boxy stairs led up the wall on their left to a closed door. Jerry led the way, followed by Maddy, then Gordon. At the top of the stairs, Jerry opened the door and Maddy followed him inside.

Maddy could feel the space below them before she could see it, a drop-off hidden in the dark. She hung back, not wanting to step over the edge until her eyes adjusted. Soon, she saw a faint, throbbing light coming from below. They were on a balcony like Jerry had said. Jerry was already standing at the railing looking down and he beckoned her over silently. Maddy walked over to Jerry's side and looked down.

The space below them was filled with candles burning in row after row, casting enormous wavering shadows on the walls. Some of the candles were moving in a line and Maddy saw that they were being carried by men walking slowly in a line toward a plain altar with only a rough wooden cross nailed or bolted to the wall. The monks all wore plain brown robes and the tops of their heads were shaved in the traditional tonsured style. One of them—Maddy couldn't see which one—was chanting words she couldn't understand but recognized as Latin, the sound of his voice made larger like his shadow in this cavernous space.

Maddy felt Jerry's hand come to rest on top of hers where it rested on the railing. "Isn't it beautiful?" he whispered in her ear. She turned and saw his tender smile and felt surprised to realize that he'd done this for her, that she was the reason he'd brought them here tonight. He'd known what she needed. For the first time she felt a surge of warmth and certainty, knowing he would be a good father.

A bell rang somewhere and all the monks joined together in the chant which was not a song but *like* a song in the way that the tone of their words seemed to reach inside her and move things, touch things. She swallowed the lump that had risen in her throat and took a deep breath, letting the sound of the monks' voices and the glow of a hundred candles take her back to a time before the terrible thing had happened, before she'd read the words that wiped out the happy memory of her mother's and father's lives. She closed her eyes and breathed in the scent of burning candles and could see her mother's face again, young and smiling and looking down at her. *Yes. Beautiful. Isn't it all so beautiful?*

The bell rang again. Maddy opened her eyes and saw four monks appear below from under the balcony, pushing wheelchairs, then two more. Elderly monks slumped in the wheelchairs, small as children, their thin bodies appearing to melt into their brown robes. The monks brought the wheelchairs down the aisle and arranged them in a line directly in front of the altar.

"They must have come from the infirmary," Jerry whispered. Maddy could see one of the elderly monks nodding his head endlessly, another with arthritic hands drawn up under his chin, trembling violently. How kind, Maddy thought. To bring these aged, sick men into this circle of light one night every year. This was how it should be.

Another bell rang. Maddy looked down and saw five more monks appear from below the balcony carrying wheelless chairs by long wooden handles. In each chair sat an ancient-looking monk, more decrepit and emaciated than the last group.

"Jeez, how old are *those* guys?" Gordon whispered.

The monks brought the chairs to the front and sat them down close to the altar. Their backs were turned but Maddy could see the profile of one seated monk illuminated against the candle light. His sunken eyes were hidden in shadow, his mouth wide open in a kind of frozen, silent howl. A string of spittle hung suspended in his open mouth.

"Wait...wait a minute," Gordon said. "What..."

Maddy looked closer and saw that what was hanging in the monk's open mouth was not spittle. It was a spider web.

"Oh Jesus," Maddy heard Gordon start to whine. "Oh God..."

"No, no..." Jerry was speaking fast in a brittle-sounding monotone. "This...this is...There are churches in Italy...This is what they do."

Maddy couldn't see the faces of the other monks seated in the front but she caught a glimpse of their hands clutching the arms of their chairs, the bones thin and fragile-looking as sticks, the skin bled dry of color and worn paper-thin.

The bell rang again. Two monks appeared carrying a wooden chest about three feet long. The chest was decorated with some kind of tarnished gold metal and studded with crude-looking gems that glowed dully in the candle light. As the two monks passed slowly with the chest, Maddy saw the other monks bow their heads, except for the ones seated in the front. The two monks set the chest down on a wooden stand in front of the altar and the chanting stopped.

"Jerry, please, let's go," she said, digging her fingers into his arm. "I want to go."

"Wait..." Jerry whispered, his eyes fixed on the scene below. "Wait..."

The two monks moved to either side of the wooden chest, undid the metal latches and lifted the lid. It took Maddy a moment to understand what she was seeing. Inside the chest on a bed of white cloth was a small child, no more than a baby, dressed in a worn-looking white and gold brocade gown. The child's mouth was open wide and the blackened gums were peeled back from the tiny yellowed teeth. In the hollow eye sockets were two large red gems that reflected the candle light and seemed to wink and move.

The bell rang one more time. Then the monks began to scream. They all stood where they were with their mouths open wide and screamed as though the skin was being flayed from their bodies. The terrible sound rose up and filled the space around her until she could not hear or speak or breath. She saw Jerry pressing his arms over his ears, his mouth moving like he was screaming too but she could not hear it. She looked for Gordon and found him huddled on the floor in a corner, clutching his head and rocking back and forth.

Without looking back, Maddy turned and ran from the balcony into the stairwell where the screaming was somehow even louder. Clutching her hands over her ears, she stumbled down the stairs and almost made it to the door before the terrible sound drove her to her knees. The screaming was coming from the walls around her and from the cold stones beneath her knees where she found herself kneeling and rocking. She knew that even if she opened the door and ran across the frozen field, the screaming would follow her; it would rise up from the ice and snow below her feet and pour down from the stars above. No matter how far she tried to run or how long she lived. The screaming was the sound that the world made and always would be.

BELOW THE FALLS

Daniel Mills

————◆————

GENTLEMEN, I AM tired of ghost stories. In my lifetime, I have heard a hundred such tales, a hundred variations on the same tired formula. We have the respectable narrator, the decrepit country house. A series of unsettling incidents: disembodied footsteps, say, or voices in the night. Finally there is the ghost itself, which bursts upon the narrator's mind like the swift and violent intrusion of the repressed id. His faith is shattered, his sanity. He is never again the same.

But there is life in the old form yet. If we take the defining quality of a ghost to be its attendant sense of mystery, its *otherness*, then I propose to you that we are surrounded by such spirits at all times whether we choose to admit it or not. In pain the mind hides even from itself, becoming a darkened star around which light bends but does not pass through.

I hope you might allow me to read from an old diary. The tale it relates is, I aver, a kind of ghost story, though the dead do not walk in its pages, except in the usual way by which the words of the deceased survive on paper long after their graves have been filled.

The diary came into my possession some years ago when I was practicing medicine in Lynn, MA. A nurse at the hospital in Danvers, knowing of my interest in psychoanalysis, mailed it to me upon the death of its author, a young woman by the name of Isabella Carr.

Mrs Carr was born in Walpole, NH, and lived there with her mother and stepfather until the age of eighteen, when she was married to Horace Carr, Esq, of Beacon Hill, Boston. The diary begins shortly after her wedding and depicts the weeks immediately prior to her committal.

Aside from these few facts, the nurse's letter was tantalizingly vague, and in the same spirit, I present the diary to you now without further prelude.

APR 2

Alfie was here again last night.

I heard him at the door, his faint scratching. He was just outside the room, waiting for that late hour when the whole of the house lay sleeping and there was only me to hear him.

I opened the door. He scuttled inside, dragging his belly on the floor. He was terribly thin, his hair all in patches. It came away in tufts beneath my fingertips, baring the pitted skin beneath, the sallow flesh speckled with rot: they had buried him alive.

I dropped to my knees and wrapped my arms around him. He did not resist but merely lay with his head against my chest as I whispered into his ear.

I'm sorry, I said. I thought you were dead.

His breathing was strained and rapid but still he did not stir. He listened as the words poured out of me, an undammed torrent. I spoke for hours, or what seemed like hours, and later, I awoke to find him gone with the bars of sunlight on my face.

Bridget woke me. She entered the room while I slept and now applies herself to the tasks of stripping the bed, taking down the curtains. She whistles as she works—an Irish song, I suppose, for I do not recognize the tune.

Downstairs, the clocks all sound the half-hour, and I know that I have overslept. Mr Carr awaits me in the breakfast room. He will be dressed for his clients, his club, checking his watch as the minutes tick past and still I do not come—

APR 7

A letter from Uncle Edmund—

This morning I woke early, before dawn, and padded downstairs in my nightgown. In the hall I found the mail where it had been dropped through the slot. In amongst my husband's correspondence was a letter addressed to me in my uncle's hand.

I recognized it at once. Edmund is my father's brother, his senior by ten years or more. He is a big man, like Father was, and likewise well-spoken, if occasionally given to maundering, and his avowed agnosticism had once made him a figure of some controversy in our household.

When Father died, Edmund took to writing me long letters, and these I cherished like jewels, for I heard my father's voice in his words and seemed to catch his scent upon the page. The letters ceased with Mother's marriage to Mr Orne, who is a Methodist of the meanest sort, though it was months before I realized they had hidden them from me.

Uncle Edmund had obtained my husband's address from a gentleman friend in Walpole "of some slight acquaintance" with Mr Carr. He rarely speaks of it, but Mr Carr was born there as well and is, in fact, my mother's cousin—though he relocated to Boston as a young man and was subsequently estranged from his family for years.

Now Edmund writes to say that Father's house has been sold and is soon to be demolished. My mother has moved with Mr Orne to Vermont, so as to be nearer his church, while our neighbors the Bosworths have bought the property. They have plans to erect a gristmill, damming the creek where it plunges to the falls.

Soon it will all be gone: the gardens, the paths down which we walked on summer evenings, Father and I, when the damp lay thickly on the air and the rosebushes rustled all round. I remember. We crossed the creek at the footbridge, where the petals lay like a blood-trail, and sat together in a place above the falls while the current frothed and broke among the rocks below.

APR 8-9

Midnight—

I hear the church bells tolling, the passing of the mail coach. An old man sings his way home, and a young girl weeps in the alley. In the silence of this hour, each sound recalls to me my shame and the solitude that followed. Days and nights in that bedroom with the curtains drawn while Mr Orne kept watch outside and Mother walked the halls, screaming.

From the bed I watched the curtains change in color from gray to yellow to crimson. On cloudless nights the moon shone through the fabric, flesh-white and glistening with grease, making stains on the bedclothes and running like an oil in the blood—

For months I listened for the swollen creek, fat with autumn rain, white water roaring as it fell. Sometimes I thought I was dying. Other nights I was certain of it. In the evenings, I heard the winds blowing outside, and Mother weeping, and Mr Orne ascending the stairs—

Then one night he unlocked the door and entered the room with his bible under his arm and the usual prayers upon his lips. He knelt beside me and took hold of my wrist. He said some words. There was a sharp pain, then, and a light washed over me, cool as spring rain or the touch of God's breath on my forehead, and finally, I slept.

APR 11

Sunday, no church—

I will not go. Mr Carr is away on business, and for all of her coaxing, Bridget could not rouse me from the bed. She is a Catholic girl, of course, and quite devout. From the window I watched her hurry off to mass, wearing her Sunday hat with the brim pulled down to her ears.

Then I dressed myself in the blue silk he had loved and sat by the window with my diary in my lap. As I write, I watch the birds circle the rooftops opposite. I admire their ease, their lightness. They drift like bracken on the churning current, carried this way and that with the wind through the chimney-pots, dropping like stones when they sight the river.

The ice is out of the Charles. Every morning reveals a surface more degraded, riven with forks of liquid water. Last week Mr Carr walked home with me after church. He was meeting a client after lunch, a young man of my own age, and was in rare good spirits. The day was fair and warm and we took the bridge over the Charles.

Halfway across, I paused and gazed down at the river with its plains of blue-gray ice and glimpsed the creek behind them like the words in a palimpsest. I could hear the falls, too, over the clatter of wheels and footsteps, and recalled the garden at night. The rush of water spilling over rocks, foaming far below. The answering hum of the blood running through me.

Mr Carr joined me at the railing. I asked him of what the ice reminded him. He thought for a moment and said that it resembled a map.

Yes, he said, more confident of himself. It is much like a map of the city. Do you see? he asked, pointing. There is my street, my house.

April 11th and the ice is gone and Mr Carr's map with it. Beacon Hill has dwindled away into the black water, and soon my father's house will follow. There will be only the river, only the creek, two channels feeding the same sea. I must go back—

APR 15

This morning at breakfast I raised the matter of the house in Walpole and asked Mr Carr for his leave to travel there. At first I thought he had not heard me, for he did not answer, and did not wrest his gaze from the newspaper.

I must see it, I said. While it is still standing.

He turned the paper over. He continued to read.

Hmm? he murmured.

Father's house, I said. Our neighbors, the Bosworths—

Mr Carr slapped down the paper.

His cheeks were flushed. They had darkened to purple and the pores stood out below his eyes. We have been married three months, but I have never before seen him angry.

And how is it you have heard of this? he demanded.

Uncle Edmund, I said. He wrote to me.

Is that so? How interesting.

He reached for his coffee cup. He sipped from it, seemingly lost in thought as a carriage passed in the street outside, rattling the buds on the trees.

He shook his head slowly. When he spoke, his voice was low and level.

He said: It is entirely out of the question.

I will be discreet, I said. Say nothing—

He slammed down his cup. The saucer cracked beneath it, upturning the cup and sending the hot liquid spilling across the table. He leapt up and called for Bridget. The girl appeared in the doorway with her eyes downcast, looking terrified.

Clean this up, he said. He indicated the mess before him.

Yes, sir.

He glared at me. Leave us, he said.

And I left—but I listened outside the door.

Mr Carr was furious with Bridget. He hissed and spat at her and threatened her dismissal. It would seem he believes that she sneaked a letter to my uncle on my behalf. The good Catholic girl, Bridget did deny the accusation, but bowed her head and accepted this punishment as her due, speaking up only to voice her agreement, and later, her apology.

See that it does not happen again, he said. Good day.

Bridget swept out in her apron and skirts. She scurried past me with her face in her hands, reaching the staircase at a near-run.

For his part Mr Carr pushed back his chair and vanished

through the opposite doorway. I heard the front door shut behind him, his footsteps on the stoop.

He will visit his club when the working day is done. He will not return for hours.

Bridget

[The next page appears to have been removed.]

I still think of it, that first sight of the Atlantic. When I was sixteen, we visited the coast south of Portland and stayed with Uncle Edmund in a cottage on the sea.

Evening fell, and we followed the reach of the shore beyond the lighthouse. By then the tide had gone out, leaving the dead fish piled all round and the great ropes of seaweed like sheaves in a summer field, waiting to be taken up and carried in.

The stench was overwhelming, sour and sweet and sharp with the tang of the sea. Father fell ill. He broke from me without warning and stumbled to the water's edge where he emptied his guts into the ocean. Afterward, he lay feverish on the cobble and muttered to himself of the battlefields of his youth: Fredericksburg, Chancellorsville.

I held his hand. I listened. The waves went out from us as the rains moved in, sweeping the shore and eclipsing the light on the rocky headland. There was thunder, then lightning, and Father stirred, moaning with the dark that lived inside him.

I shook him, gently. Father, I said.

He opened his eyes.

APR 19, 5 O'CLOCK—

I have seen to everything. It can do no harm now to write of it.

The carpet-bag is packed and secreted beneath the bed, and I am alone, waiting for Bridget to return. She left the house at noon to pawn my wedding ring. With the money she will purchase two tickets for a northbound train that will bring us to Walpole in the morning.

Tomorrow! I am frayed and shaking, a cord drawn taut. I can smell the old garden, the roses. The scent is more vivid in memory than it was in life, mingled with the perfume of soil and damp and that of the blooming linden. I close my eyes and hear the creek, sending up spray where it drops beneath the bridge, and remember the great clouds of dragonflies and the way they drew near us at dusk, wings flashing—

LATER—

I am locked in. The door is shut, the key turned fast.

Bridget has betrayed me. She now keeps watch outside, walking up and down the hallway and singing to herself in Irish. Moonlight spills in a fan across the floorboards, shining on broken glass and specks of hanging dust. I had time only to hide this diary before Mr Carr stormed inside with Bridget following him meekly.

He was livid, incandescent with rage. He swept the bottles of my medicine from the dressing table and stomped down on the remnants, grinding the glass beneath his shoes.

Bridget retrieved the carpet-bag from under the bed. At first I thought she meant to spare it his fury, but instead, she merely placed it wordlessly into his hands. He snarled and tossed the bag on the fire. The fabric caught light, then the clothes inside, the blue silk Father loved—

I threw myself at the fireplace, but Mr Carr caught me by the wrists and pushed me to the floor at his feet. Throughout this time he said nothing, but his eyes were black and shrunken to points, like those of Mr Orne, when he ministered to me in the dark of that winter, or those of my mother when first she found us out in sin—

Mr Carr produced his ring from his coat-pocket and jammed it down the middle-finger of my left hand, forcing it past the joint so I knew I should not be free of it.

You made a promise, he said. To me as I did to your mother. We mustn't forget that.

Come, he said to Bridget, and they were gone.

APR 21?

Mr Orne is here. He paces beyond the door. In his tread I hear the echo of steps from long ago and imagine the house in Walpole where I watch the faceless mourners come and go.

Some hold dresses or kitchen implements, bed-sheets caked with red and yellow filth. One man carries the charred remnants of my carpet-bag while another walks with fistfuls of broken glass, blood dripping from his hands. They proceed with unearthly slowness, with all the gravity of pallbearers: rolling up the rugs, wheeling out the cradle, carrying off the materials of home like the seashell spoils of some god-conquering army.

Now the house stands empty. It is a ghost of itself, an absence made visible, like the clothes Father wore that morning, when he left the house, and which the Bosworth boy found above the falls. They were neatly laid out, the boy said, the pants folded in quarters, the wedding ring left in his shoe.

That ring: its smoothness on my skin. Whatever became of it? After the funeral, when the mourners had gone, Mother plucked the band from her own finger and flung it into the creek, as though to sink Father's memory with it, and now I am her cousin's wife.

The lamp is dim. Mr Carr's ring glitters. It casts a white smear on the wall, an inverted shadow which moves in time with the rhythm of my hand on the paper so that I think of the moon in Maine as it rose over the headland, dragging the waves behind it, water and light trapped in the song they sang between them until at last you woke and looked at me—

Dusk when I reach Walpole. From the station I walk to the house, lifting my skirts and sprinting when I hear the singing creek.

I am too late. Little remains save rubble. The floors have been torn out, the walls collapsed into the cellar, and the garden, too, has been plowed under.

The flowers are gone, the rosebushes. Uprooted and piled on the brush heap. Burned. The smell of wood-smoke lodges like cotton in my throat, stopping the air in my lungs. I can't breathe—can't walk—a fever is on me—

It pulls like the spring current. It drags me through the ruined garden on hands and knees and down the path that leads to the footbridge. Here the water ripples, waves within waves. The creek is running high. Below the falls the waters teem with light, the glint of gold like the flash of drowned skin. Mother's ring—or yours—and my blue dress charred and floating—

This was where it happened, where they found you.

Alfie is in the hall. I hear him scratching. I must

THE DIARY ENDS there. The remaining pages are blank.

In those days, my interest in the abnormalities of the human brain took me to Danvers at least once a month. On my next visit, I sought out the nurse who had sent the diary.

She was a young woman of pretty coloring and sensitive disposition. She was, in fact, nothing at all like the matronly figure I had imagined. I gathered that she had been quite close to Isabella Carr and considered herself to be something much nearer a friend than a caretaker. She thanked me for coming, and for my kindness in reading the diary, and showed me into the room, as yet vacant, in which Mrs Carr had lived out the final years of her life.

From the nurse, I learned that Mrs Carr had been committed by her husband following an incident in their Beacon Hill home in which the family's Irish maidservant had been attacked and nearly killed. Edmund Ashe had contested the committal order on his niece's behalf but his efforts failed when evidence of opiate dependency came to light.

Throughout her time in the hospital, Isabella was never seen to write letters or keep a diary but instead spent her days beside the window, absorbed in silent contemplation of the grounds below. When she was twenty-eight, she sickened with pneumonia and died. Afterward the nurse found the diary tucked up inside the lining of the feather-bed, where it had languished, apparently forgotten, since Mrs Carr's arrival at Danvers some years previously.

"I'm not ashamed to say that it gave me the chills," the nurse said. "For a moment I even imagined that she had wanted me to find it. Nonsense, of course. She was ill. Probably she had hidden it inside the bed and forgotten about it. Of course it should have been sent to her family—her mother, if not her stepfather—but after reading it…well, it didn't seem right, somehow. And Edmund Ashe is dead these two years."

"Had she no other family?"

"No," she said. "She hadn't."

Her eyes moved over the empty walls and she was suddenly far away.

"It's sad, really. As I said, her uncle tried to fight the committal order. In the courts it emerged that Isabella had mothered a child some years previously, a little boy. She was unmarried at the time, and it had all been hushed up. Her mother and stepfather conspired to hide the pregnancy from their neighbors and married her off to Horace Carr soon afterward. He was Mrs Orne's cousin, as you know, a man of certain habits, and it was rumored that the marriage had not been consummated."

"And the little boy? What became of the child?"

"He went to an orphanage. A woman came by and carried him away. I don't believe Isabella ever recovered from that—though I was often uncertain of how much she remembered. In any case, the poor babe didn't see his first birthday. Cholera, I believe it was."

"What was his name?" I asked. "The baby's."

She did not answer me immediately. Instead, she went to the window and closed the curtains halfway, drawing a shadow across the bed. She filed from the room but paused in the doorway to address me a final time.

"The child's name," she said, "was Alfred."

She disappeared into the hallway. Her footsteps retreated down the corridor. The sun broke through the parted curtains, and I was alone with my thoughts.

THE KEEP

Kirsty Logan

———— • ————

WE STARTED WITH a ring. We thought she would like that. When she opened the drawer and saw the ring there, reclining gleamingly on a hank of pink silk, her face opened up sunny-joyful. We knew that she thought it was from him. That couldn't be helped.

She put it straight onto her finger. We watched her toy cattish with it for the rest of the day, twisting it to and fro as she swooned and hummed around the caravan. When she'd first arrived she'd moved slyfoot, placed teacups down with fretting care, each step tightroping. We knew why. When we'd first arrived, we'd seen the way the little tin caravan sat high in the tree, bound to the thick oak branches, hung flimsy-like over a fast-flowing burn. We'd all moved slyfoot then too, at first. We did not want to make the caravan fall clatter-crash out of the tree. But soon we settled, just as she was settled, and her steps fell hard as hail. That was when we crept out of our hiding places.

To and fro, to and fro she twisted the ring. She cleaned in time with her songs, finding pretty nooks for all the things that needed tidying away. A pint of milk, a pink slinking nightgown, a dustpan, a pair of toothbrushes. The caravan was a labyrinth of hidings: drawers and cupboards and little sneaky nooks. Finally she felt the words spark scratchy on her skin. She frowned, pulling off the ring to peer at its innards. *Until I die.* She rubbed where the etched words had caught her. *If we had had breath, we would have held it.*

We watched her frown a realization, then release it in fear of wrinkles. We knew as well as she did that he would not stand for wrinkles. Perhaps the ring was not a gift from him after all. Perhaps she'd stumbled on the remnants of old loves. But whose? *Until I die*—he was still alive.

She tried to open the drawer and re-secret the ring. But that drawer would not open again today. She tugged and she coaxed, but the drawer stuck fast. Finally she hid the ring in her face-cream, dropping it in and shaking the little pot until it was submerged. We watched as she opened and opened and opened the bathroom cupboards until she found one the perfect size, its edges kissing the face-cream pot as she slid it in. Such tininess in the caravan, but always somewhere to be secret.

When he came home, she greeted him with neat kisses. We hid in the smallest cupboard and listened. There was no talk of gifts. Her finger was swollen where the words had scratched, but he did not notice. Outside the caravan, the rain shushed and the wind throbbed and the moon blinked bright. Inside, time stopped. The chattering burn stole all sound; the spreading leaves took all sight.

After dinner, he used his petty magic to transform the couch into their bed. They lay together. We wished that we still had hands, so that we could cover our ears.

THE NEXT DAY, after he had left, we tried again. A hair ribbon. Plush velvet, thick as wolf-fur, red as a heart. She found it while trying drawers in search of washing-up gloves. She forgot about the dishes and reached for the ribbon. It curled lovingly into her hand, and with a turn she bumped the drawer shut with her hip. She pulled back her conker-shining curls with one hand, the other ribbon-busy.

But—a tickle on her fingersides. She stopped and peered. Three hairs twist-tangled in the ribbon, ever so long and ever so blonde. We watched her look at the hairs. We watched her stroke the blood-red ribbon. We watched her fingers come away wet. With a cry she dropped the ribbon and kicked it away from her.

She didn't try to open the drawer again this time. She knotted and knotted and knotted the ribbon and she opened her underwear drawer and pushed it right to the corner, covering it up with her fripperies and frills.

When he came home they ate in silence. Her fingertips were stained red. They went to bed, and we had no need of covering our ears. In the darkness we heard the click-clack of her thoughts.

WE WATCHED HER open the drawer four more times in four more days. We left her a silken negligee delicate as mothwings, a pair of stockings twisted garrotte-thin, eyelashes faded grey and crumbling, painted fingernails with fleshly scraps caught at their bases. And on the seventh day, we left her a heart.

We watched her open the drawer like she was looking into a lion's mouth. She'd turned slyfoot again. Despite the labyrinthing, she was running out of places to hide our things. She pulled back when she saw the heart, enthroned in the drawer among a scatter of dried roses. It shivered in a single beat. She leaned in. Perhaps she thought it was a kitten, butter-soft and full of mewls. Perhaps all these gifts were from him after all.

We watched her lift out the heart. She held it in her hands. She squeezed it. Hard. The flesh bulged around her fingers. Of course she did not think it was a kitten. Now we understood her thoughts and her insides as if her skin was made of glass.

He'd taken a caravan, a portable shelter, ordinary as dirt—he'd taken it and magicked it into a labyrinth for girls, a make-believe home the size of eight coffins lashed together. Some girls escaped, but we didn't. We ignored the signs, or the signs weren't there. We'd got lost and we'd never been found. Our tangles of hair, our bright scraps of frock: tossed up into the trees, to be worked into birds' nests. Our straight white bones and our tender mauve organs: dropped down into the burn, carried out to sea. He thought that was the end of us.

She spoke to us then. She told how he had found her. Rescued her. Claimed her. Made her see that the world was cold and dark and hard and empty—but with him, life would be delicious, abundant. He put his hands over her eyes, and when he took them away she saw differently. The happenings before him were too hard to focus on, furled and dark like sun-damaged film. All she could see was his face.

We know, we cried, though she could not hear. We all knew his face. It was the last thing we'd seen. We shouted that it would be the last thing she'd see too. He'd tear out her heart just so he could hold it in his hands. He'd throw the remnants of her to the trees and the sea.

Some of them ran long before reaching the heart. Some of them ignored its urgent throb, staying until they couldn't leave. But for her, this was enough. She dropped the heart. With her bloodied hands, she tore open the door. She ran away.

We knew she wouldn't be back. We slipped back into the littlest cupboards and waited for him to come back to his crowded, empty home.

She Rose From the Water

Kyle Yadlosky

———◆———

"She needs to be dead," the grey-suit preacher tells Laura. He sips coffee; his lips slurp against the rim of the cup. The tip of his tongue runs along his off-white mustache, lapping up what's left of the coffee's bitter moisture. He sets the stained white mug on the dining room table. Laura sits across from him in some dingy three-day worn dress. She nods and pushes limp, unkempt curls from her sweating forehead. She hasn't bathed in weeks. She has nowhere left to wash herself.

"You don't float four days and come out breathing. She ought to be dead," the preacher repeats and waves a finger toward Laura's neck. She nods, stares red-rimmed eyes at her legs. Her lids beat. The dining room chair creaks as the grey-suit preacher adjusts his weight. "Folks throw around words, you know. It ain't true. I know miracles. Even little girls aren't always brought back by a holy hand. Do you understand? Other forces work under that skin."

The preacher pushes his cold coffee to the middle of the table, and Laura's eyes catch the ripple of coffee lapping against the inside of the mug. It beats the rim, threatening to spill over onto the table.

Waves pound rocks. Wind chills her shoulders; she bundles her wrap closer behind her head. The police lead her to the edge of the rocks. Camera lights flash. Voices babble under waves. The officer's hand squeezes her wrist. A finger points toward the water. Voices babble. Eyes watch. Her ankles bend, feet easing over loose rock. A flashlight raises; a white orb shines on glistening stone just at the edge of the water. Laura holds her breath. The voices babble; the waves batter. The finger points. She nods. She stares as the wind dries and burns her eyes at her daughter's little green shoe sitting sideways at the edge of the water. She collapses to her knees and lets the rocks scrape her skin, chisel blood from her legs. She screams into her hands; she cries. The waves batter over her cries. The voices babble on as a mother slashes her fists, beating them against the loose rocks.

The preacher glances to the ceiling. His eyes hold the beams. "No daughter up there," he murmurs. "She left you with the current. Mark my words. No daughter up there."

Four days she had no daughter, until a flannel fisherman took his boat in early waters so still that he slid across them like glass. Through the low fog he caught sight of strands of hair, closed eyes, blue lips.

Laura's eyes rise from her thighs to the door frame of the dining room and peer into the dark living room. Knocks pound the main door. She opens, and that fisherman stands with a pale girl hanging in his arms. This girl lies, eyes closed, under a brown blanket. He takes off his hat, smiles. Laura sets her little girl in bed. In an hour the girl opens her eyes. The grey-suit preacher and a bow-tie doctor stand to Laura's sides, looking over the girl. She vomits water for an hour into the bathtub, filling a pink-grey liquid into the tub until the water beats the edges. She sleeps for three days. The bow-tie doctor assures Laura that she has no need to worry, that the daughter will sleep. She'll be dehydrated when she wakes up. Laura must be sure to keep plenty of fluids on hand.

When the daughter wakes, a crowd circles the house.

"Water is life," the preacher grumbles. "Nothing holy up there.

Whatever it is, it's trying to take God's place. You know that well as I do. She spilled her life inside that tub. Let me do what needs to be done. Let me do what you know is right."

Laura nods. She watches her knees, only hears the preacher's chair creak, his grunt. His shadow climbs the door frame as his body twists and his lower back cracks. He straightens, sighs. "I'm glad a woman like you could come to her senses." He rests a rough hand on her shoulder. It drives a chill into her spine. He stretches his sides and coughs into his fist. "Well, then. Best be done with it before we change our minds."

His heavy shoes thump up every step, beating through the walls and ceiling of the house. His labored breathing rises and falls like waves pounding rocks with growing force. The floorboards creak as he lumbers down a hallway. Laura's eyes follow the creaking. A knob rattles, door opens. The grey-suit preacher's voice rings muffled. "Come now, little one"—a bed creaks—"I won't hurt you. I promise. I won't hurt you." The floorboards sound heavy steps back down the hall toward the staircase and farther down. Laura watches the ceiling. Her sweaty palms run back and forth over the skirt of her dress. Another door opens. Feet pound into a small bathroom. Water ripples. "Still warm," she hears the preacher murmur.

The water ripples in the hot afternoon. The house rocks with wet heat; hundreds of bodies shuffling close together, talking, chanting, stifling every room. Laura stands in a corner, watches. Her little girl runs down the stairs handing each body a strip of paper where a number's been scrawled in black ink. She taps wrists, reassures people. Then, she bounds up the stairs to the bathroom. She calls out a number, and a body creaks up those stairs, down that hall, and to her daughter. Laura only watches the ceiling from her corner in the dining room. Voices rise. Songs bellow out. "Oh, sweet angel. Oh, child save me. The pain is too much. Oh, surely you see. Oh, sweet angel. Oh, daughter of grace. You are the savior. Of our human race."

The songs skitter like bugs under Laura's skin. Hands clap; the noise bores through the walls, fills the dead air like the bodies through the house. Laura closes her eyes. She sweats, gasps. She screams, but the song tears her voice away. She jabs a finger, but no one sees. She stomps her foot, but the clapping vibrates her house to the foundation. She shouts to leave her home, to leave her child alone, but her daughter's praise crushes her outrage.

She slaps a man waiting at the stairs, shakes him by the shirt. He only thanks her for bringing such an angel to the world. She looks to the stairs. She knows she could run up them; she could grab her daughter by the wrist; she could escape what her house has become; she could save them both. But there's something about going up there, about seeing her girl doing whatever magic she now possesses, that twists Laura's guts.

"She rose from the water. And will rise as planned. When the great storms come. And swallow the land."

Every face floats down the stairway, peeled to a clown's grin. The pink-grey water of the bathtub drips off each chin, and every voice adds to the choir, belting a new hymn of their child savior. Laura holds her hands over her ears, closes her eyes, and crouches in the corner. The house shakes under her feet. The house trembles like the walls might split, the foundation might crumble. This tuning fork to her daughter's sacrilege, she wishes it would crumble. But it stands; it will always stand. An old woman paints a portrait on the wall. Laura knows the golden curls of her daughter's hair, the olive eyes. The woman dabs angel wings onto the girl, singing on with the crowd.

Laura's head rings too much, head rattles too hard, so she wanders from her at-one-time home in search of a preacher's guidance.

The house stands still now. The walls wait, holding breath. The first splashes come. The little girl screams. She screams again. Water sloshes onto the floor just overhead. Laura watches the ceiling. The screams rise. The floor creaks. The grey-suit preacher belts out, "Now, unholy demon, monster of sin, you shall not hold this home captive! You shall not poison the faces of those searching for salvation! You shall not lead sheep astray from the

Lord of Heaven! You shall return to Hell! You shall return!"

The floor creaks; the walls shake. Her little girl screams and gurgles on deep gulps of grey-pink water. The preacher stomps his feet, holding her down. "Back to the water!" His voice pounds through the house. "Back to the water! Back! Back to Hell!"

A stain grows over the dining room ceiling. The spot stretches dark in an oblong pool. The floor creaks, walls bang. The screams ring under water. Splashes break off the side of the tub and fall in downpours. The stain grows darker. A drop of water falls, splashes into the preacher's mug. Laura follows another drop. And another.

"Back to Hell! You will not poison this woman! You will not poison her home! The devil has no foothold on Earth! Back to Hell! Back to Hell and tell him so yourself!"

The screams ring out, and the drips break to a stream. It pours quickly into the mug. The coffee rises and spills black across the rim. Black runs over the sides and pools across the table, then trickles onto the floor.

Her daughter stands on the floor, head barely higher than the dining room table. A green swimming cap holds her long locks back. She smiles at her mother and kicks her green shoes. Laura looks out the window. Grey clouds pull across the sky, churning the coming storm. The heat is high, and the sweat makes her daughter itch. She just wants to swim it off. Laura leans down to hug her little girl, kisses her forehead. Just an hour. No longer. It'll start to rain after, and dinner will be ready.

Laura watches her daughter from the doorway, running down the path toward the beach.

The splashing slows, stops. The screams die. The preacher breathes. His shoes squeak from the bathroom and thump through the hallway, pound down the stairs. He nods to Laura, his face beating red and eyes standing wide. He has no words left in him, so he lumbers through the dining room, opens the front door, shuts it behind himself, and never glances back at the once-upon-a-time mother. The house falls back to silence, except for the steady trickle of bathwater falling from the dining room ceiling.

Laura doesn't move. She sits stiff and watches as the grey-suit preacher's mug continues to overflow and spill her daughter's grey-pink water. Her eyes float back to the ceiling, knowing that in the room just over her head, her daughter floats dead.

Warm bathwater sloshes as Laura screams. A man with a dark face grips her hand, holds it tight. He pets her hair, whispers in her ear. He'll be gone in a few days time, but for now his voice calms her as she pushes this body out of her stomach. The man rubs her hair. "Just one more. One more. She's on her way out."

Laura grunts and cries out. She pulls her eyes closed. The bathwater spills onto the floor. The man whispers in her ear. She pushes, and a weight releases from between her straining muscles. The water splashes. Laura opens her eyes. Another involuntary shudder of her body, and the afterbirth follows. The man lets go of her hand.

The water is cloudy and grey, and the red of her blood and fluids has dispersed through the tub. She breathes and pants. She doesn't hear a baby scream.

The man dips his hands into the water. He pulls the baby up. He rocks it; he pats its back, but the infant makes no sound. Laura, exhausted and lost, begins to weep for her lost child and for the fruitlessness of all her pain.

The man continues to pat the infant's back, and it coughs. It spits up a trickle of water onto the floor. It spits again, it gasps, and it starts to cry. Laura looks to her baby, and the man rests the newborn in her arms. She rocks it gently and continues to weep.

The baby looks up at her, and it croons. It splashes a hand into the murky water her mother made and reaches up. It runs its fingers over her mother's face and paints all the tears away with that grey-pink water.

ANIMALHOUSE

Clint Smith

——————— ◆ ———————

There are times when the lines around the human eye seem like
shelves of eroded stone and when the staring eye itself strikes us
with such a wilderness of animal feeling that we are at a loss.

"The Country Husband," John Cheever

THE UNEVEN SERRATIONS *of the house key scrape into the front
door's deadbolt like teeth tumbling over bone. He twists the knob. A
forearm netted with dark, dried blood rises and shoves the door,
which glides open.*

*When he'd left earlier that morning, Gary Mountjoy had neglected
to pull the blinds. Now, near-evening light glows throughout the house,
casting sharp shadows, as if someone has done a negligent job of
hanging dark blue wallpaper.*

*His fever is insistent—nearly as assertive as the pulsing pain within
his arm. Then there is the matter of the body in the trunk of the car.*

Priorities.

NASHTON WAS CLOSE, about twelve miles away.

It was that twelve miles that separated where he'd grown up—

in the fielded outskirts of Nashton—and the suburbs with which he identified his current existence.

Courtney had left town the day before—to visit her family, she'd said…to take some time to think, she'd said—and his wife's abrupt two-or-three day absence presented Gary the perfect opportunity to do some thinking of his own, which is precisely why he decided to dismiss much thinking altogether, opting to call in sick to work and spend Monday daydrunk alone.

Well, not alone. He had Gamble.

The morning's checklist had contained two items, both of which had been enthusiastically exed-off: Call in sick to work and drop by the liquor store for a bottle.

As Gary drove further into rural stomping grounds, the radius became more tolerable, more enjoyable. It was during this time of seasonal transition when the leaves were turning, altering from green states to tints of nectar, rust, lemon, uncountable tinges of orange. The roads became more narrow, the trees lining those thoroughfares became more prominent, dense.

An atmosphere insulated with Rorschach stretches of forests and cordoned fields, now set in tall stands of harvest-ready cornstalks.

He'd never been one to denigrate his former stomping grounds— not that he'd ever intentionally reside here again. Nevertheless, he identified with Nashton.

Gary grew up out here in an area that had four vital set-pieces in his formative years—forests, farm houses, fields, and railroad tracks which cut through the center of this place as a sort of carotid landmark—the steel rails a symbol of the bygone days when locomotives brought people here. For a brief period in the mid-nineteenth century, this small community was poised to rival towns in their campaign to become Indiana's state capital. That candle of ambition, though, guttered in light of other community campaigns. It was a matter of not being big enough, not being *rich* enough. *A matter of not being enough.*

Oh yes, Gary Mountjoy identified with good old Nashton. *Nice try…better luck next time.*

As a sentimental exercise, Gary took a detour through the town itself. Ghost town was too much of a cliché, though it did seem like some sort of campy re-enactment could occur at any moment. Outside the diner were two filthy men smoking, perhaps accosting patrons for a handout. *The railroad's doing*, Gary thought. Back in the old days, there'd been stories of rail-riders, hobos hopping off as the train slowed or stopped at Nashton's depot. Stories of wayside vagrants creeping through the community, wandering from yard to yard, or casually soliciting folks for a handout or a hitch out of town.

The two men held their beady gazes on Gary's car, their faces containing a mummified sort of dignity.

Toward the southeast, the railway eventually connected with Cincinnati, and on toward the northwest met up with the spider-web network of Chicago.

The elementary school he'd attended as a kid was still out here, yet had been shut down due to some funding issue which spurred a shift in district lines and transportation. Now, kids who were supposed to attend Nashton Elementary were being fed to the nearby and slightly larger town of New Bethel.

Gary pulled into the front lot of the now lifeless school, appraising the low-lying, one-story structure with its mannequin-composed facade—no boards over the windows, no broken glass, just absent energy. He continued his circuit around to the back of the school, the secluded side screening him from the town proper.

Gary slowed to a stop, Gamble already huffing, panting, drooling, mincing an anticipatory dance in the confines of the backseat, his ID tag jingling against the clip on his collar.

Courtney, when she'd walk Gamble around their subdivision, had consistently used a leash on the animal.

Gary glanced over on the passenger seat—the leash there, more of a perfunctory tool than a necessity. Gamble was clumsily kind, oafishly obedient.

Next to the leash was the brown bag. He'd never taken a day off from work for an illness, let alone as an excuse to get drunk as a means of self-pity capitulation.

Gary craned his neck, wondering of the possible presence of some security guard or errant maintenance man on the grounds, before slipping the bottle from the bag, paper crackling as he withdrew the pint of bourbon. He gazed at the warm, amber-hued liquid, catching sight of his long, gourd-distorted reflection along the edge of the bottle.

Gary peeled away the plastic ring and twisted the cap, the whiff of distillation filling the space. He again glanced around the deserted back lot before raising the bottle to his lips and taking a small pull. He winced, grateful no other males were present to provide any sort of casual shaming. Gary allowed the liquid to descend, savoring the swift-spreading scorch as it traveled down to his empty stomach. Inhaling, exhaling, Gary immediately followed up with a larger gulp, which was better after the previous primer. He wiped his lower lip with the cuff of his windbreaker. The physical thrill of absorbing the spirits mixed with the deviant awareness that he should be at work right now—being respon-sible, being a teacher of children. He thought about the marriage counseling, about the guy at Courtney's office. His mind cut to the chase; he wouldn't, couldn't, rehash the details. There were only so many ways to depict domestic depravity.

Gary took one more sip. It was shaping up to be a beautiful morning.

Gamble was whimpering now, his nails tapping at the window frame.

Gary capped the bottle, took a deep breath, and stepped out of the car. Still midmorning, the sun slowly adding thin layers of warmth, he went up on tip-toes, stretching his arms, the move-ment felt as if he were allowing the alcohol into far-reaching cells of muscle fiber. He peeled off his windbreaker and tossed it on the driver's seat, rolling up the sleeves of his flannel.

Gary scanned the parking lot of the elementary school, the ad-joining playground with its rusted array of disused and outdated equipment. There was a small baseball field on the far side, now overgrown, weeds and ivy crawling up the chainlink backstop. Hemming the school in on the west side of the property was the ever-present railroad tracks, which separated the property from the ever-present fields and forest. Up beyond that, set on a small bluff overlooking the tracks, was the house.

When they were students here, Gary and the other kids called the house "Corpse Cottage," though it was evident that, back then, it was inhabited by a family. Prone to typical embellishment—no one had ever died there, no crime (of which Gary was aware) had ever taken place.

Later, when high school boredom compelled teens to country-side excursions, Corpse Cottage became a regular haunt. Of course by this time the house was clearly abandoned—shingles sloughing off the ragged roof...paint peeling in oak-leaf-size portions. As a child, Gary'd heard tales that the house had been a hideout for transients and squatters from the railroad. Not for the first time he acknowledged that the house's location—set up on a low-sloping bluff, almost hanging over the tracks—would be ideal for transients searching for a place to seek shelter. Gary stared at the house, its gray exterior covered with a netting of limb and autumn-leaf shadow.

Gamble barked sharply. Gary flinched. "Sorry about that, old boy," he said, opening the back door.

Tongue lolling, the dog spilled out of the car and trotted across the parking lot, panting, pausing to sniff the air, Gamble's collar and ID tag jangling as he ran, roaming a curious weave throughout the skeletal playground.

Gary took the opportunity to reach back in through the open window and pluck the bottle off the seat, giving panoramic appraisal—nothing, of course...everything in the school yard fringes was tranquil, desolate. He swallowed and looked at the bottle, startled by how little liquid remained.

Carl, their therapist—or marriage counselor or whatever humiliating term was being used at one time or another—had suggested during one of their sessions that adultery was really

about anger. This initially baffled Gary. For two reasons really—
one, he had no idea what his spoiled-to-the-marrow wife had to
be angry about; and two, if he were indeed the source of that
anger, then what the fuck had he done precisely?

He shook his head, already feeling the gliding, gut-warming
sensation of inebriation. *Need to take a break, pal.* He capped the
bottle and nestled it beneath the driver's seat.

Gary glanced toward the playground. No dog. The only thing
moving was a tepidly swaying swing.

He straightened, eyes darting. "*Gamble!*" he shouted, stepping
away from the car. Gary cupped his palm to his mouth. "*Gamble!*"
The word skipped, doubling on itself as the echo drifted across
school grounds.

Gary heard him before he saw him. In the distance came the
metallic jangle of the dog's ID tag. Gary swiveled in the direction
of the baseball diamond. Gamble was nosing around the weed-
threaded backstop, tail wagging, inspecting the space where home
plate would be.

Gary sighed, half-smiling as he looped the leash around his
knuckles and started slowly for the baseball field. Keeping his
eyes on the dog, he mumbled, "All right, bud, enough fun…
time to go."

Though Gary hadn't raised his voice, Gamble raised his head—
ears erect, the set of the animal's body suddenly rigid. His muzzle
pointed directly at Gary, two black eyes staring. He actually
chuckled. "Sorry, my man…but we'll have plenty of days to run
around at the park."

His voice held the intonation of a father speaking to a child.
Like most young couples, everything was a "starter"—starter
home…starter savings account. Starter pet in preparation for a
starter family.

They'd never articulated the dynamic, that taking care of a dog
was a tacit-collaborative barometer for their parental potential as
nurturers. But they'd sensed it, particularly when Gamble was a
pup. Though, as Gamble aged, he became more of a prop in a

two-person play. As time went by, Gary was more and more at a loss for how the script read.

Closing in on the dog now, Gary considered his limited threshold for the thespian nature of noble husband—his wife had crossed the line. She'd made groveling attempts to apologize, which Gary summarily rejected, only accepting the invitation to counseling as a matter of pre-separation perfunctory. Courtney had sworn it was a one-time mistake—something she regretted and could not account for.

The dog's legs were set sturdy beneath it. Slowly, it lowered its head, its upper lip curling to show the warning gleam of teeth. A low rumble.

Gary didn't come to a full stop but slowed a bit. "Gamble?" he said, some disbelief at this strange response from the gentle dog. Gary stifled the urge to raise his hands in a plaintive gesture. He just needed to get close enough to attach the leash. Soothing: "You want to stay a while, we'll stay a while—okay?"

Gamble, as if stung by something on the hindquarters, twitched, breaking its stare with its approaching owner and whirling in the opposite direction. The dog froze.

Gary did too. Scowling, he examined the outer stretches of the property, out beyond to where the dog had now trained its attention; but before he could gather any sense about what had happened, Gamble barked once and bolted, taking off toward the railroad tracks.

Gary hissed, "Damn it," and began chasing the dog in a dead sprint.

"*Gamble!*" Gary called out, the sun warm on his neck and shoulders. Gary reached the tracks, but the precariousness of the large rocks and wooden ties slowed him a bit. He shouted the dog's name again just as the animal veered left into the underbrush, loping up the steep slope toward the house.

It took Gary a few seconds to catch up to where the dog had cleaved through the weeds, leaves made hashing sounds, wand-thin branches snapped as Gary ungracefully navigated the incline of the small bluff, finally pushing against the bole of some anemic trees to get his footing where the ground leveled off in the refuse-littered backyard. Panting, he almost shouted again, but could hear the dog's rapid barking—it sounded as though it were coming from inside the house. For just a second, Gary thought he heard a reedy whistle.

He frantically scanned the exterior. All details, of course, were worse up close (a lesson he'd learned from his demanding in-quiries into Courtney's adulterous dalliance). Three-stories worth of neglect—flaking paint exposed scuffed planks...sagging gutters overloaded with dead leaves and debris led to fractured downspouts barely clinging to the side of the house. The grounds were littered with an assortment of age-varied trash. Again, like a stuttery newsreel, Gary thought of the rumors that this place had once been a stopover for train-hopping transients. The crooked railing on the L-shaped porch contained broken or missing spin-dles, and except for the very high attic dormer, all window glass was missing, each transom broken.

Jogging, Gary rounded the side yard, trying to determine where the dog had gained access. On the back end of the house was a partly open door. He pressed against the door—some resistance there. Pressing harder, shoving with his upper body and craning his neck to see what was on the other side, he saw that two duffle bags—faded green, the Army fatigue variety—were stacked against the door, but had been scooted away, providing a narrow margin of access.

He shoved the door and slid into a narrow corridor, still hearing the dog's barking—*Damn it...he's upstairs.*

The smell of engine oil was heavy here; and the idea of oil was a pervasive thing—whereas a tint of sepia tiredness may seem noble in some cases, here it imparted a sense that the nicotine-tinted surfaces were coated in grease. A filmy, hibernating scent of nesting insects.

The sound of movement up on the second story—capering claws clicking on the floor overhead. "Come on, Gamble...get your silly ass out here," Gary called out, using the most author-itative tone he could conjure. He began clapping his hands together and whistling as he walked toward the deeper interior of the house, shattered plaster and dead-leaf detritus crunched under his sneakers.

Though the windows were bare, little light seemed to filter into the shadow-curtained house. Just as Gary was about to emerge from the corridor, Gamble abruptly stopped barking. Gary held his breath involuntarily. After a few seconds of silence he said, "Gamble?" Quiet. Gary strode forward and around the corner.

Just a few feet to the left was a staircase, flanked on one side by a wall and a broken railing on the other.

The dog was standing at the top of the stairs. Gamble's body was crisply profiled with his attention trained on something to the left. (The dog could have been an insignia on one of Puckett's designer shirts, the notion coming as a mental sneer.) Now, Gary's voice was nearly a growl. He placed one foot on a riser and said, "Damn it, *Gam*—"

From the second floor came a string of short whistles, each ending with an unsettling chain of cheery notes. Gamble's growling reemerged, grinding up to reverberate down the stairwell.

With his hand on the wobbly railing, Gary almost swayed when the whistling ended with a series of sloppy kissing sounds —a male voice, threaded with something unsteady—said, *"Come over here, Gamble…"*

Skittering as the dog sprang forward, nails clacking and scrap-ing. Gary followed, pounding up the stairs.

The commotion was to the left, at the end of a long, shadowed hallway. Gary bounded into the passageway, all doors were closed here, allowing for insufficient light through the rectangle tunnel.

Gamble was on top of someone—a struggling figure, one fore-arm angled over his face.

Gary kicked through garbage and newspapers, getting within reaching distance of Gamble and the person he was attempting to maul. He leaned in and grabbed Gamble by his collar, the band of fabric vibrating against the dog's growl-rattling throat. As Gary was struggling to peel the dog away, he caught a better glimpse of the feeble-framed, rag-clad figure.

Just then one of the man's arms shot out, thin fingers clutching the dog's collar.

Gary assumed the man was simply trying to gain leverage to get to his feet, but the pull was strange. Gary slid an arm under the dog's neck, trying to get between the two, almost immediately feeling the slick sting of teeth in the flesh of his forearm, Gamble's snapping jaws snagging on skin. Gary cried out, heaving backward, and in one tug-of-war lunge tore the dog loose. He landed hard on his hip—Gamble still growling, still flailing—and skidded back into the hallway and into the light, not far from the stairway corridor. Still holding the dog in a sort of feeble bear-hug, Gary got his legs to the staircase, looking over only once: a mistake which forced him to falter.

The man was sliding on all fours. As he emerged into a weak shaft of light, Gary first noticed that the guy's skin was pallid, waxy-gray, a tint associated with wasting disease. His fever-rheumy eyes glittering in deep-set sockets ringed dark, as if he'd been rubbing his eyes with coal-dusted fingers. Nearly bald, a few oily strands, resembling limp silk from a sick cornhusk, clung to his pate.

The man's cracked lips were smile-stretched, the grin show-casing a rotted cavern of mouth—Gary's attention was arrested by this detail: his front teeth, the incisors, were missing, but on either side of the gap the canines were shockingly long and sharp.

Gary's terror-pause at seeing the man had been too much. Like most revelations, the ability to immediately rectify his errors came far too late. The sick man edged forward, his long, filth-grimed fingers grabbing the dog by the collar. The smell coming from the man was something from a flesh-fouled trench. Gary tried to scream as he watched the man, almost playfully, open his lip-cracked mouth—the missing incisors making everything more black there—the long, sharp canines—and watched the man's jaws close on the dog's throat, petals of blood blossoming on fur.

Gamble yelped—a sharp, helpless sound that renewed Gary's strength and he hoisted.

The dog's collar snapped in the sick man's hand as Gary fell backward, Gamble in his arms, both tumbling down the stairs. They hit the floor hard, though still Gary hefted the dog to his chest and broke into a shuffling run toward the door.

They spilled into the yard. Fresh air—Gary sucked in the late-morning air, staggering, rounding the house on his way to the bluff and the tracks.

The sound of laughing. Gary twisted, his eyes tracing the laughter to a second-story window. The sick man was standing there, smiling, chin smudged with blood. Those teeth—the missing incisors…the pronounced, rot-tinted canines.

Gary winced—from the weight of the animal, from exhaustion—as the man lifted his hand, the dog's collar dangling there, Gamble's silver ID badge catching sunlight—a jolly ornament. The man's expression bore a taunting sort of intent.

Gary turned, doing his best to manage the steep hill and the thick undergrowth along the bluff, sliding the final six feet down the slope. He glanced down at the blood-matted fur along Gamble's neck, crimson glistening in the sunlight. Then the railroad tracks were underfoot, racing over the ties and thick stones.

The run across the baseball field was a mishmash of panting and nonsensical encouragements: *Hold on, old boy…few more… car…get you patched up…*

And then they were there—Gary sweating, breathing taxed. He gently laid Gamble in the shadow of the car, trying to keep the dog comfortable. The dog's respiration had gone wheezy. Gary reached over, suddenly seized at the sight of blood trailing from his own arm. In the struggle Gary had been nipped by Gamble—*no—not right*. Gary whirled around, clawing at the back door of the car to retrieve a bottle of water; he uncapped it and poured the liquid over his forearm. Clearing away the blood validated the worst—the puncture wound now clear, literally in his flesh: a ragged bite…two distinct canine punctures with a gap between.

His mouth was dry. It hadn't been Gamble. His eyes darted around, lighting on playground equipment, acres of harvest-ready fields. The ruined house up on the bluff above the train tracks. He sunk down to one knee, pouring the remaining water over Gamble's neck. Useless. A wide pool of blood had gathered under the dog's upper body. Breathing had stopped.

A barbed ripple of pain pulsed along his forearm. The water bottle in his hand was empty—*the bottle*. Gary yanked at the passenger side door of the car, retrieving the bottle of bourbon from beneath the seat. He was clueless whether it would help, still he fumbled the cap off and poured the liquid over the wound—an electrifying sting forked along his ulna.

Gritting his teeth, he dropped the empty glass bottle, swiped an old t-shirt from the trunk and wrapped it around his arm, falling back on his backside against the side of the car and sliding down to a seated crouch.

Thoughts—*call a sheriff…call an ambulance*—fluttered in the weak breeze of his mind. The one that stood out was Courtney—how was he going to tell her what had happened.

Losing the dog. Eyelids shuddering, Gary tried to focus on the rotting house in the distance, his attention eventually falling to the playground equipment as his vision began to blur, beads of sweat glistening on his brow. And as he slid sideways, his eyes closed, accepting the tightly scoping darkness on the fringes of his vision, Gary Mountjoy heard the hush and hiss of the breeze in the trees, the wailing sound of a distant train threaded in the wind.

WE'VE EXPLAINED ALREADY—it was a pretty unexceptional entrance.

IT WAS VERY near dark now.

He was thirsty—the need for water was demanding. He'd have to get the shovel soon.

As Gary shambled through the house he noticed that his vision was pretty good, adjusting to the dimness with crisp swiftness.

The bleeding had stopped, a smear of dark, resin-like liquid crusted over the wound; but, for the moment, Gary could not allow himself to focus on the teeth marks, what they meant. *Human teeth.* He was worried about infection. Unbidden, the word *further* spasmed through his mind. *Better be worried about further infection, my friend.*

Earlier, back at the school, he'd woken disoriented, sprawled on the asphalt. The first wave of flies had mingled around Gamble, and Gary batted them away. He ripped open several garbage bags, spreading out a piecemeal tarp in the trunk, gently lowering the dog into the space. With his hand lifted to the trunk's lid, Gary paused for a moment, reverentially considering the animal. No matter what he would tell Courtney, this physical thing that had linked them was now gone.

Now, he teetered toward the bathroom, taking a swipe at the light and instantly regretting it. The figure reflected in the bathroom mirror was a double-exposed version of Gary Mountjoy—tall, lean, but the exterior had frayed. Gaunt—his skin was ashen, if not downright gray, and was pulled tightly over his eye sockets, cheekbones. Facial stubble had grown to several-days-worth, and his damp bangs hung in a coarse curtain over his brow.

His eyes skittered to his forearm, but before he could remove the knotted portion of t-shirt, he wondered at the coarse, whisker-thick hairs coating his muscle-corded forearms. He brought his dark-nailed fingers up and unwound the piece of blood-crusted fabric. That was when Gary noticed his fingernails, rimmed with dark tints, as if stained with mulberry juice. And they'd elongated as well, converging to sharp points.

The bite marks were livid, each puncture haloed by a dark network of tendril-like bruises; and though the punctures had ceased bleeding, the dots where his skin had been broken looked to now be surfaced by a thin layer of tissue, as if the wound itself had sunken a few centimeters deeper into his arm. *A hematoma tattoo.* Gary barked a laugh aloud, his lips drawing back—again he caught sight of himself in the mirror: teeth: his upper and lower canines had lengthened, like slender tusks, curving toward each other.

Gary reached over and swiped off the light, pitching back into the hallway in a half-crouch.

Gamble. He had to do something. *Priorities, pal. A good suburban soldier had priorities.*

He grabbed an old comforter from the closet, opened the garage door and backed the car in.

He had the decency to wait for the sun to disappear.

BURYING THE DOG was a series of stuttery, strobe-light stills. In the woods out back, Gary eventually discarded the shovel, digging Gamble's grave with long-nailed hands. The growls grew louder as the pit got deeper.

BACK IN THE house, he was coated in a fine film of dirt. He felt as though his fever was beginning to abate, but the pockets of ache remained, particularly along his sternum and spine.

His ears popped, as if from a pressure change, just before he felt another shift as something popped along his jawline. Breathing heavy, Gary clenched his teeth and found they didn't line up quite right.

He tried to rise to full height and failed, discovering that remaining hunkered over slightly elicited less postural pain.

Keys. Gary staggered into the garage, fell into the driver's seat and jammed the car keys into the ignition with a jittery-clawed hand.

Of course, during the months of obsessive questioning—of both his wife's infidelity and his own self-worth—Gary had discovered where Ryan Puckett lived, had even driven by the house once or twice, juxtaposing his life with that of the guy compromising his wife, a self-flagellating exercise which did everything to confirm the young man's vulgar display of income.

Gary would just go over and talk to this fellow. This guy had fucked Gary's wife, apparently. Having a civil, man-to-man discussion was not out of the question. After all, Gary wasn't a total animal.

HE PARKED THE car down the street from Ryan Puckett's house.

He had no plan, didn't even begin thinking about what he'd do until he was out of the car and shuffling up the sidewalk. A gray Lexus sat in the driveway, its engine still ticking as it settled from some recent outing.

Gary scanned the front of the house—the meticulously manicured lawn, fussy landscaping, precious accent lighting warming the unblemished structure. Gary had a flash of regret, wishing that when he'd been in college studying to be a common, parochial teacher, he would have known he'd never be able to afford such an opulent property. Which also reminded him that he would certainly be calling in sick again tomorrow.

Mustering what dignity he could—his filthy flannel shirt smudged with soil—Gary skulked up the driveway. Stepping into the light of the front porch threw Gary's slouched shadow against white brick—the silhouette resembled something like an upright hyena...the sharp nails flexing, as if each were competing for his attention.

Through cloudy glass, light shone in a distant room. Thoughts fluttered into his mind like agitated bats: *Courtney's in there— she's lied about going to visit her family—her car's in the garage— they're in there right now—in the bedroom—in the dark—in her...*

A gray, hairy, knob-knuckled hand extended toward the doorbell, a black claw touching the amber button.

A sing-songy tune sounded from within, the cheerful melody triggering a wave of pain, this one coursing across his ribs, sending him reeling. With a pain-lashed squint, Gary sneered and threw his shoulder against the door, producing a brilliant *crack*, a noise he enjoyed. This time—*in her*—heaving heavily, Gary backed up a few paces before throwing his entire weight into the act: hinges splinter-ripped away from the frame, the force of his momentum causing him to follow through, spilling onto the entryway's laminate floor.

A scream was just beginning to die away, and Gary glimpsed a figure—female—retreating toward the inner light of the house. His molars fused, he clawed at the hardwood and broken glass as he hunkered down and pursued.

He made one rushing leap, stretching out through midair, and took a swipe at her, missing her leg by an inch before landing on his side. Gary scrambled to his feet, rounding the corner of the great room at the same moment that Ryan Puckett—mouth ajar, eyes bugged, chest hitching—stopped short by the arm of the couch.

A very large TV was playing some evening game show. Gary could smell the savory scents of dinner, synthetic air freshener— the "normal" aromas accented just how bad he smelled: fever-soured, mangy, dense. He didn't belong here, which was even more reason for him to stay.

Still stooped, Gary managed to raise up a bit, feeling cords and connective tissues yawn, joints pop. Felt good. He flexed and wriggled his claw-bayonetted fingers, showed Puckett a double row of deadly teeth and took a step toward.

Puckett's mouth was working to say something, but all he could manage was a sort of preface to a question—"*Whu… whua…wha…*"

He tried to make an evasive move but collided with the end table, a lamp pitched over, light and shadows swirling as it hit the floor.

Gary clutched Puckett by the nape of the neck, nails snagging on Puckett's dress shirt, and shoved him over the couch. Gary rounded the side of the couch and loomed over Puckett, who now, with an outstretched hand, was working on a word: *Guh-Guh.* Gary raised a claw and took a swipe at the raised hand, the long nails connecting with flesh, leaving a four-lined laceration along the man's hand. The financial advisor cried out.

Gary didn't hesitate—his claw-splayed hand shot down toward

Puckett's chest, grounding him into the thick carpet while the other hand rose over his head in a contracting, nail-hooked fist, and prepared to bring it down somewhere along his face to mar the—somehow even in terror—magazine-handsome features.

Only then did it occur to him that the screaming had continued this entire time. Over on the far side of the room next to the fireplace. Gary spared a glance and paused.

He saw the woman's face first, thin fingers drawn over her open mouth as she whimpered in short bursts. A blonde, willowy, faked-tanned thing. Not Courtney.

On some rational plane, Gary registered that Courtney had mentioned this during one of his domestic inquisitions—Puckett had a wife; it's just that Gary never devoted much care to the detail. But now, a rabid-ruthless thought emerged—*How would you like it if it happened to your wife, Puckett? Fair's fair, friend...*

Kids. Two of them. A boy and a girl. Both huddled at the waist of their shrieking mother, who clearly intended to place her body in between the children and the hyena-shaped thing in the living room.

The little girl's face was slicked with tears. The boy's expression was nearly impassive—something idling in the gears of terror, anger, and awe. The game show continued its inane banter as a soundtrack to the wife's shriektrack.

There were a pair of patio doors on the opposite side of the room. The glass there—Gary, with the lamplight distorting the shadow angles in the room, caught sight of his reflection. His upper body had taken on a hunched slope, his arms, which terminated in those black talons, appeared too long for his body. The angles of his face, particularly his nose and jaw, were out of proportion. His gray skin was barely visible under patches of excessive hair.

Gary shivered, his lemon-formaldehyde eyes skimming the room—the abrupt, preparatory movement caused the room to go quiet, the whimpering and crying ceasing for a moment. All those glittering, helpless eyes were set on the tall thing in the center of the room. From within his aching ribcage, Gary produced a guttural noise that slowly climbed to a long, grating growl. Gary raised his face and let loose a wall-quaking scream.

He stopped and looked down at Puckett, who had been an inch away, his bleeding hand still extended as a pathetic sort of defense. The woman had pulled the kids in tighter behind her, almost sitting on them now. Gary's upper lip twitched back from his sharp teeth, as he reached down and grasped the overturned tablelamp, flinging it across the room and into the massive television—a thousand sparklers ignited and faded, the room dimmed to darkness.

Gary's chest rose and fell in furious bursts as he twisted and lumbered out of the family room, out of the home. He left them, crying together in the dark.

THE CAR WAS nearly impossible to drive. Not because Gary was incapable—he still felt as though most, *most*, of his faculty remained intact—but because his body wasn't fitting right, his knees awkwardly raised on either side of the steering wheel…his curved spine—which continued to give the occasional achy *pop*—felt uncomfortable against the seat. He dismissed the seatbelt, entertaining himself with the notion that it was no better than a leash. *Human leash*, he mused. *Leash. Collar. ID badge.* The transient standing in the window, standing there holding the dog collar with a lunatic triumph, the silver disc of the ID badge catching some of the sunlight.

Gary swerved a bit as a nagging revelation gained clarity.

In his mind, he summoned the scene from earlier—the man standing at the window with the dog collar raised; but now his imagination tightened in on the ID badge itself, the silver disc containing the engraving of Gary's phone number…their home address. *Courtney.*

There was still a portion of Gary that recognized what was going on. He was sick, an illness incrementally braising his brain. When he tried to articulate a cogent narrative for what had happened and what he needed to do, his left-brain impulses folded over themselves, replaced by a smoldering sensation that everything was being transformed into a sort of fuel. His ribcage connected to his spinal cord like piston headers feeding some deep, growling combustion.

No matter what, there was no returning from tonight. Puckett had, of course, recognized him. He could drive until he ran out of gas—he'd been driving for a while as it was, and he was now back on narrow, country roads—but then what? The flickering portion of his rational mind followed that the deterioration would continue.

Maybe she was telling the truth. Maybe it was a mistake—a one-time thing with Puckett. Maybe she was sorry. *Maybe.*

Thinking about the two of them together again conjured a new image: of mauling them, of tearing them down to puzzle-size pieces.

A violent surge of pain swept through him, his body contorted and he lost control of the car, which swerved once before careening to the left, carving two deep furrows in the soil before canting into a deep ditch and jouncing up, colliding with an anemic tree.

With steam hissing from the hood, Gary waited for the pain to die down. He should have worn a seatbelt. Again, a yipping, jackal laughter.

But when that settled, Gary was still left with one of the last, cogent thoughts—Courtney. *If the feral man has the ID badge, he could find us.* Gary automatically corrected himself. *He could find* her.

Gary sneered and lashed out, kicking at the glass of the passenger-side window which shattered. Gary crawled out of the car, his flannel shirt catching on some of the broken glass and shredding the material. Gary clawed at it, ripping the shirt away from his deformed—newformed—body.

He came down on all fours and began loping across field-lined countryside. Nashton was only a few miles away.

GARY USED HIS sprinting momentum to crash through the front door of the house—the decrepit panel exploding in a burst of tinder splinters.

The staircase corridor was up ahead. He could smell him up there. Gary rounded the corner, placing his long forearms on the risers. The feral was standing up at the top, a black shape etched in deeper darkness. The figure emitted a warning sort of mewl, but Gary was already pounding up the stairs.

He burst through the threshold, colliding with the feral, the two spilling into the hallway. Gary got his claws up under the man's armpits and thrust him against the wall, plaster cracking behind the feral, who was snarling, taking swipes with his own claws.

Gary shifted, flinging the man to the floor, his body skidding into an open area between the rooms. It took him a moment, but the feral got to a crouching, defensive position. Gary was slung low, his back curved high; as he rose with his forelimbs spread, the feral man dodged, simultaneously slashing at Gary's midsection. Gary yowled, his claws going to the searing laceration beneath his ribs.

Instead of following up, the feral attempted to make a retreat, scrambling for the hallway and the stairwell. But Gary pivoted, leaping, smashing down against him, squashing his body to the floor. Something jingled in the feral's back pocket. Tamping down his squirming body with one claw-splayed hand, Gary picked at the back pocket of the filthy jeans, withdrawing Gamble's red collar, the silver disc of the ID tag.

The feral man was trying to twist around—when he tried speaking his voice was a husky rasp: "Hunters," said the feral, "hunters…"

Gary thought there might be a fraternal sort of plea in his tone, the consideration followed by a surge of fury as Gary opened his mouth and brought his face down to the nape of the feral's neck, his long canines piercing flesh and muscle. A high-pitched yelp tore out of the feral man. Jaw still set, Gary pressed down and pulled his face away, ripping a belt of trapezium tissue with him.

Gary spit it out, sneered, and went to work again.

SOME TIME LATER, Gary staggered to the broken, second-floor window, clutching the dog collar in his gore-streaked claw.

The window gave directly on to a wide portion of roof which looked over the scrub-covered gully and the railroad tracks. Gary, his side still searing from the wound, gingerly gripped the sill and crawled out onto the shingled overhang.

He found a comfortable spot with his back against the siding. Light from the moon, which came in patches, occasionally touching the tangled-lattice treetops.

When he'd caught his breath he looked down at the object in his blood-glistening hand. The collar and ID badge. Gary rubbed the silver disc with what used to be his thumb. Gamble's name. His address. *Their* address. Relief—like black water stilling in a deep well—settled in him. Relief—as he imagined the feral inspired to track him down, to search him out and find the house…to find Courtney—braided itself with regret, for not having done more…as a husband, as a teacher.

Gary clutched the leash and tag, easing the back of his vulpine head against the house.

Time glided sideways with the phantom-cowled clouds. He shot up suddenly, fully conscious, ears perked to the eerie echo of the train whistle. He scanned the horizon. In the distance, a single light—like a phantom lantern gliding through knotted vines—stuttered behind the stands of trees lining the gullied tracks.

His yellow eyes traced the tracks north, those lines stitching through stretches of flat farmland in northern Indiana, cutting through affluent suburbs before terminating in an industrial region just outside Chicago. She was up there with her family. Maybe Courtney was really sincere about the things she'd said— about the desire to make things right. Gary still thought he should have taken a bite out of Puckett.

He looked down at the yard, his yellow eyes gauging the distance between the house and the tracks. He stood as best he could in his newly accustomed hyena posture and started huffing in both anticipation and an aching call to mobilization.

Staggering at first he began trotting across the flimsy roof, gaining momentum. He growled, baring sharp teeth as he reached the edge and sprang, arcing over the yard, descending toward the gully-shouldered tracks.

As he fell Gary caught a glimpse of the moon, unobscured now as the coal-smoke clouds had drifted away. He kept his animal eyes trained on it—sneering at that bone-colored disc even as he hit the tracks, his brindle-furred body collapsing in a heap, the train's whistle banshee blaring, the locomotive's quaking light rushing on, eclipsing the moon.

TOOTH, TONGUE, AND CLAW

Damien Angelica Walters

———◆———

ONCE UPON A *time there was a monster. This is how they tell you the story starts. This is a lie.*

HE ISN'T CRUEL, and he didn't eat her.

She isn't sure if that's a kindness or not. She isn't sure of anything but the locks and the keys and the secret scream hiding in her throat. And the last is suspect; sometimes it tastes like laughter.

But she's still alive. She tells herself this means something.

He tugs on the tether attached to the chain around her neck. A gentle tug, but it's enough. His claws click on the stones of the rocky path leading away from the cave, toward the town, a sound like chattering teeth, and although the bottoms of his feet are thick and leathery, she feels every jagged edge, every sharp point, beneath the soles of her satin slippers. He moves lightly for his size; beneath his steps, the ground merely quivers. She takes a few steps until he stops again.

People stand on either side of the path. A few wear smiles, but most carry only relief on their faces. They all know what she did, of course.

The gazes touch, linger, penetrate. She wants to scream that they have no idea what it's like—how can they?—but she won't. Even if she could, they wouldn't care. All the faces belong to strangers, but even if they were her people, they would extend neither hand nor choice.

She's on display so they know she's still among them. So they know they're safe. Does he want them to know he didn't tear her head from her shoulders, rip her limbs from her torso and toss the pieces aside? He has that right. He's had that right since the day she was given to him.

They don't do that anymore, her mother said time and time again. Her eyes said otherwise.

Or does he want to merely assure them that she did not succeed, that his power is still nothing to be trifled with, to be challenged? Yes, she thinks. It's apparent in the set of his jaw, the carriage of his spine.

She keeps her chin raised, too, so they don't forget she was strong enough to try.

LIES ARE LIKE *bits of straw. At first, there's only one; it would be easy to pick it up, break it in two, bring the pieces out into the light. But then you add a second, and you can't find a way to dislodge one without the other. A third, a fourth, a fifth, and soon the weight of the pile is impossible. It becomes a maze with no solution.*

Best to pretend it's truth, not a tangle of fiction.

WHEN THEY RETURN inside, he closes the iron gate set deep into the stone. Locks it. Closes the outer door. Locks it, too. Then the inner door. When that lock clicks, he slips the key ring onto a chain around his neck, the same sort of chain that circles hers, yet she doesn't fool herself into believing he's a prisoner, too.

LIE #1: *This is a great honor.*

HE DOESN'T TOUCH her once they are in bed. He has before and he was as gentle as possible; she knows he wants to again and in time, he will. No one told her about that part. That was a kindness.

On her side, she stares at the bedcurtains. They're heavy and embroidered with gilt like everything else in his home. (She refuses to call it hers. She never will.) Strange that monsters would adore such finery, or perhaps it is only her monster that cares for such things.

Her bed at home had no such curtains; the walls were not covered in tapestries, yet she would trade all the gilt in the world for the chance to return. She presses her face into the pillow, willing away the impossible dream.

One hand sneaks up to the chain around her neck. The links are small and delicate, but a chain is still a chain; it marks her as a possession, a *thing*, not a person.

THERE IS NEITHER *spell nor curse to break. This is not a love story. He will always be a monster; she will always be chained.*

IN THE MORNING, he touches the side of her face with one of his claws. She doesn't lean into his touch, nor does she pull away. She keeps her face impassive.

His eyes are the color of leaves beneath an early twilight sky. He speaks mainly in his native tongue—all grunts and hisses, rolling growls and throaty sounds that remind her of a cat when its head is scratched, but he does speak the language of humans as well, even though the words sound as if they're spoken through a mouthful of river stones.

Though many have tried, no human has ever deciphered the language of monsters. Who can say if things would be different if they had.

He leaves the bed chamber without touching her again, though he pauses briefly in the arched doorway; perhaps the pause is only her imagination.

She wishes she could be content, because it would be so much easier. For her, for him, for everyone. This is the way it's supposed to be. This is the way it's been ever since the monsters awoke from their deep slumber and claimed their place in the world as leaders of men and beasts alike. This is the possibility for every secondborn daughter, something she was taught from the moment she was capable of learning.

Why she isn't content, she doesn't know.

(Maybe the others aren't content either.)

AFTER THE DRAWING, while the councilmen waited outside, her mother brushed her hair for a long time without speaking, without meeting her eyes. She thought she heard a faint whisper, a muffled *I'm sorry*.

Maybe it's only what she wishes was said.

He brushes her hair now, the silvered handle awkward in his grip. She closes her eyes, pretends she is still a child, pretends it's her mother's hand holding the brush. But the breath touching the back of her neck and the smell of him tells her the truth.

LIE #2: *In time, you will forget your old life and come to embrace the new.*

HIS FACE, FORELEGS, and belly are heavily scarred from the fight with his siblings and sire for the right to rule.

Eventually, he, too, will sire young and when the males reach full maturity, they will challenge him for the right to rule. The last left alive will rule until it becomes time again to sire and fight. (She will be long gone before then; the monsters live a lifetime equivalent to that of five humans.)

A barbaric practice, to be sure. Yet is it any more barbaric than humans tossing an etched stone into a pot to select a random girl who must become a monster's consort, all in the name of peace?

THERE IS A story she and her friends (and how she misses them most of all) told each other—of someone like her and something like him and love, love enough to break the chains, to not care of the consequences, and they would sigh and fall back, staring up at ceiling or sky, daydreaming of a love so powerful and beautiful.

But they were young and knew nothing of monsters.

WHEN HE IS not there, she walks the cave—from wide open rooms to narrow passageways that serve no purpose. The carpets (even in the useless passageways) are soft underfoot, turning her steps to mere whispers.

There are books, but secondborn daughters are no longer taught to read until they pass the age of the drawing. Still, she likes to open the heavy tomes, breathe in the pages, pretend she under-stands the words. She thinks of her friends learning letters and words and stories, and her hands fist tight enough to hurt.

Be brave is the last thing she remembers her mother saying.

But she isn't brave. Stealing keys and trying to creep out in the middle of the night is foolish, not brave. Everyone knows monsters have exceptional hearing; she knew she wouldn't get away.

And she doesn't want to be brave. She wants to be free. She will never learn to be content, she will never stop dreaming of life outside the cave, and she shouldn't have to. She refuses to.

She puts her face in her hands, not to hide her tears, but to hold in her rage.

LIE #3: *As a second daughter, your natural born duty is the safety and security of others.*

IN THE MORNING, he reaches for her face. She pulls away. He stares, considering her, for a long time, his eyes inscrutable, but he doesn't reach again.

When he leaves, she hides her smile behind a palm. A small victory, but a victory nonetheless.

THE COUNCIL KEPT her drugged, something she only realized when she woke alone on a dais, surrounded by flowers of a type she'd never seen, the entrance of the cave an open mouth, her own mouth still throbbing with pain. She heard his approach and refused to cower, refused to close her eyes. Her wrists and ankles were bound; even if she'd wanted to run away, she wouldn't have been able to.

He was not as bad as she'd imagined. He was also worse.

THE CENTER OF the cave holds a pool surrounded by rocks worn smooth by the passage of many monstrous steps. The water is deep and always warm, and she spends many afternoons there, floating on her back, staring at a circular hole in the stone high overhead—the only break in the outer cave walls not locked and barred.

Today, though, she doesn't disrobe. Instead, she runs her hands over the pitted walls and gazes at the hole.

She reaches high, curls her fingers into a gap in the stone, does the same with her other hand. Finds a toehold, pulls herself up. Not quite like climbing the trees as she did when a child, but near enough. Reach, pull. Reach, pull. Until she finds nothing but smooth surface, no nook or cranny for even one finger. With a sigh, she eases down and moves to another spot.

Although she climbs higher this time, she reaches a spot where she can't quite grasp the next handhold, no matter how hard she strains, willing her spine to lengthen, her arms to stretch. She tries again and again until her palms are scraped and raw. Back on solid ground, she rubs her hands together, relishing the pain as she lets her gaze span the rest of the walls.

Tomorrow, she'll try again. She isn't sure how she'll manage to traverse the top, where it begins to curve toward the hole, even if she reaches that far. Maybe she'll simply tumble into the water below or perhaps to her death on the rocky path.

HE TOUCHES HER palms gingerly. His eyes ask questions that his mouth does not, questions he knows will go unanswered save for clumsy pantomime, and she's in no mood for games of any kind.

When he pushes her down on the bed, she presses against his massive chest, and shakes her head hard.

Again, he pushes. Again, she shakes her head. He growls but he storms from the room, his every step leaving behind a heavy thump.

She doesn't bother to hide her smile.

LIE #4: *They cut out your tongue so your voice, your words, will not anger him.*

HE IGNORES HER for several days.

She climbs the walls near the pool, each time ascending higher and higher. She inspects the bars in every window and every doorway, testing for weakness. The discontent inside her grows like an unborn babe.

Do any of the others feel this way? And what of those who came before? The stories, the histories, say no. They say all the girls handed over to the beasts were honored and treasured, but who can say for sure. Who knows who truly wrote the stories.

Was Livia of Northingate gifted with furs and diamonds? Did Rebecca of Southton have the most magnificent library ever built? (This was before they decided secondborn daughters should not know how to read and write.)

In spite of the finery, they were all prisoners still. The stories didn't say that; they didn't have to.

Her mother said eventually she would grow to be happy. (Barring the other option of ending up between teeth and jaws, of course.) But her mother was a firstborn daughter. She never had to worry; she was never to be given to a monster.

Is *he* content? Why wouldn't he be? He doesn't sacrifice, he doesn't pay with silence and disfigurement, he doesn't pay at all.

So why should she?

HE TAKES HER shoulders, lowers his face to hers, pushes her back toward the bed. Holding out her hands, she makes a sound that isn't a word but wants to be. He steps back, his face wary, unsure, ghosted by a touch of anger.

She holds her breath, but meets his gaze with her own. Will he kill her? One slash of his claws could split the skin of her neck, sever her head from her shoulders; one snap of his jaw could tear apart her body from nape to tailbone.

He exhales loudly, gives her his back, and, after a long moment, leaves the room, trailing the echo of a growl. She sinks to her knees, her heart racing. Although she doesn't want to live this way, she doesn't want to die.

How many others have shared this cave with him and what happened to them? Did they dash themselves to pieces on rocks while climbing to an illusion of escape? Did their lives end in his gullet? Did they grow old and aged and infirm?

The stories never tell of such things. But no one knows because no one ever comes back. They're never allowed to. To do so would break the agreements—ancient ones written in old languages no one can speak anymore.

The words may very well be lies themselves.

SHE TOUCHES HER mouth; feels the weight of forced silence. *Her* people did this. *Her* people allowed this to happen. No, encouraged it. Her silence and captivity ensured their safety so they were more than willing to do whatever was necessary.

This is not for the monsters' sakes, but for theirs.

When they delivered her into the hands of the council, did they weep or simply erase her name from their lips and her face from their memories as though she were dead, not imprisoned? Did it help them sleep the sleep of the just and dreamless at night?

Would that she could haunt their nightmares, turn their own voices to screams.

LIE #5: *He is the monster.*

SHE CLIMBS. HER shoulders don't ache as much as they did when she made her first attempt. Hand over hand, she rises, moving her body to the side to reach new handholds. So intent is she on her progress, she doesn't hear him enter the room, only becomes aware of his presence when he grabs her around the waist, and plucks her from the wall as a child plucks a blossom from its stem.

Instead of dashing her against the rock, he lowers his arm and lets her drop. She lands on her side with a jolt; her teeth clamp together, the sound like a snapping twig. He bends down until his face is inches away from hers and roars. She recoils from the noise, from the heat and stink of his breath, and then he's gone.

Hands shaking, she sits beside the pool, willing herself not to cry and failing, miserably so.

THAT NIGHT, SHE pushes him away with all her might, fights as long and as hard as she can, but he's stronger. Damn him, damn them all.

A day later, the hole in the cave wall above the pool bears a set of bars.

These are emphatic messages that speak louder than any voice could project—she belongs to him, and the only way out is death.

EVERY NIGHT, SHE fights. Every day, she ignores him and pretends the bars don't exist. She climbs, bloodying her palms, tearing her clothes. In the hallways that lead to nowhere, she paces and wills herself to stop thinking of the outside, to stop thinking of choices and hope, to be content. But she can't live this way, not without going mad. Would that he would do her the kindness of killing her, of ending it all.

Sometimes she dreams of his teeth tearing her flesh, ripping her into tiny pieces. Other nights, she dreams of someone breaking through the bars, rushing in to sweep her away, but in the morning, the lie fades away. No one will save her from the monster. No one will take that risk.

They never have. They never will.

FINALLY, SHE REACHES the top of the wall, where it begins to curve. With one hand firmly grasping the edge of a small cleft and her toes tucked into two more, she extends her free hand, fingers dancing across the rock in a gentle waltz. Here and there, she finds gaps, spaces she's sure she could grip to swing herself across to the window.

She flexes her hand and takes a deep breath. A sound darts through the air. Tightening her hold, she peers over one shoulder to see him there, his massive body reclining against the wall. The sound comes again, and it takes her a moment to place it—laughter. The largest insult of them all. Her face blooms with heat; her mouth twists.

No more, she thinks. No more.

IN A NARROW hallway, she finds a loose chunk of stone the size of her hand, one end wide, the other narrowing to a jagged point, and tests it against her palm. As pearls of red bubble to the surface, she smiles, but there are tears in her eyes.

She waits until the middle of the night, until the cave fills with the sound of his slumber. On her knees with heels resting against the back of her thighs, she lifts her arms, brings them down. The jagged point of the stone parts scales and sinew, and blood runs crimson and warm down his neck. His eyes open. He roars and extends his claws; pain flares in her upper arm, but she doesn't stop. She can't. And there's so much blood. Rivers—oceans—of it. Hands slick, her mouth filled with the taste of wet metal, she stabs again and again and again until her breath is ragged, until his is no more.

Sobbing, she drops the stone and wraps her arms around her knees. Will they flay the flesh from her bones? Pummel her with rocks? Merely give her to another monster?

No. She will not allow the latter. She strips off her nightgown and uses it to scrub the tears from her cheeks and the blood from her skin.

His body is heavy, but she manages to drag it to the floor nonetheless, and she works through the rest of the night, cutting away the pelt, carefully scraping the fat and the meat free. Using strands of her hair braided with strips of the beast's gut, she sews the rents from the stone. She rips the heart from the carcass and smears the clotted blood on her skin; then she curls her body into the hide, pulls it around her, and slips her hands into the paws.

Her flesh warms, melts into the pelt until there is no way to know where one ends and the other begins. Her muscles flex and expand, growing to fit a new shape, a new purpose. Her bones break and knit back together in a stronger construction. There is no pain, but she isn't surprised; she's already paid a thousand times over.

She opens her reshaped mouth and what emerges is neither the mewl of a tongueless girl nor the roar of a monster, but the triumph of a great and terrible beauty. All around her, the colors are brighter, the edges sharper. She gets to her feet and heads toward the entrance of the cave, trailing her claws along the walls, cutting gouges in the stone. Her new form isn't ponderous, but graceful. Powerful.

And she remembers.

She remembers the council handing her over without a second thought. She remembers everyone standing outside, watching her led with tether and chain. She remembers their gazes upon her and their silence. Peace, they called it. She has a different word for what they've done.

Emerging into the sunlight, she throws her head back, cries out to the sky. The ground trembles fury beneath her feet, and she bares her new teeth.

The people want a monster. She'll give them one.

ONCE UPON A *time there was a girl…*

MOMMA

Eric J. Guignard

————◆————

MOMMA ASKED, "WHERE'S William?"

"He's visiting Poppa," Daniel replied.

She smiled, thin lips straining upwards like a rusty lock that turns in creaks. Poppa died twenty years ago, said to be murdered during the night by a man of town who was never named. So it was true, in a way, that William *was* visiting Poppa. William was Daniel's brother and had been caught in a fire that burned him so bad, he died a week later, coughing out the ashes of his lungs. That was six years past, when Momma's illness began, when her memory began to falter. Even *she* was unable to save him.

"It's strange, the things that come to me like ghosts in my mind," she said quietly. "They appear and vanish with a whisper, as if apparitions of something I once knew. I search for them, but I don't know what I'm looking for. I don't remember what it is I've even forgotten." Her eyelids fluttered and sagged over milky eyes.

Her mental clarity was better today than it had been all week. Daniel thought he should feel relief, even some joy, at her cognizance, but instead felt only melancholy. He could not decide which was preferred: To dream blissfully unaware of what you have become, or to have recognition of the slow death sentence, the incurable disease that sweeps away your faculties.

Momma sat in a wicker-back chair under the afternoon sun. Her eyes closed, and a drool of pepper-flecked saliva leaked from the corner of her mouth. It dripped slowly down her chin, following the canal of a wrinkle, like a drop of molasses seeping from bark. Such was her mind, too, like a reservoir which leaked the sap of life, drop by slow drop, until one day it would be left as only a dry husk.

That day was soon to be coming, and Daniel felt conflicting sorrow and relief.

He kissed the top of her head and hobbled through the screen door into their house. The sounds of wood flies and cicadas followed inside. The house was dark and old, an intimate realm of musty dreams and stale woes. He walked upon its cracked linoleum, some sections missing entirely to reveal the charcoal-brushed timber underneath. In the kitchen he boiled Momma's tea, as he did five times a day. Into it he soaked wood root, gathered from mangroves out back, and added a teaspoon of pepper and a pinch of ground calcite.

He retraced his steps across the cracked linoleum and returned outside to give Momma her tea.

"Lucas, you spilled my gum oil," she said, her words slow and unsteady.

"It's me, Momma. I'm Daniel."

"I know who you are, Lucas. Get your brothers, it's bedtime."

"I will. You know they can't sleep until they say they love you."

She smiled at that and sighed, the sound like wind blowing through dead stalks of wheat.

"Drink your tea," Daniel said. He held her shaking hand in his own and guided the cup to her mouth.

She drank, and they were silent for a long time. There were no other brothers left to say they loved her. Daniel tried to make up for it, and often he would say *I love you, Momma* seven times, once for each of her sons.

Momma suddenly remembered. "They're all dead…" she said. "God, why have I lived so long?"

Daniel squeezed her shoulder with his good right hand. His left arm was shriveled and hung loose, like a parasitic thing sucking at his shoulder. The afternoon sun began to fall and the sky darkened, indigo blue, streaked with cherub-red.

He was the youngest son, born last and born deformed and weak. Each of his six brothers had been beautiful and strong as the wild sycamores that blossomed on their land. It was as if by the time Daniel was birthed, all the resources which went into making flawless children had been used up by his siblings; there was little left, and he was cobbled together with the scraps of placenta and hope.

But as each brother grew into manhood, he left their home to make his mark on the world, only to be stolen away by a great divine theft. William, the eldest, was first. Ezekiel was next, crushed by falling rock from a mudslide. Aaron was mauled by a wild animal. Lucas, struck by lightning. Henry, pulled under the dark currents of a river's undertow. Orlie, infected by raging fever. The brothers died one per year, in the order they were born.

Momma stood abruptly and hurled her cup of tea across the porch. It shattered midair into flying ceramic bits. Daniel winced. She spun at him and her milky eyes turned black as oil.

"It's the townspeople's fault. I'll get them, Daniel, every one of them," she said, her voice a rasping growl. The exertion made her faint, and she collapsed back into the wicker chair just as quick as she'd stood.

Daniel bent down and wrapped his arms around her tight. He rested his head against her breast and said, "I know we will."

She looked at him, her face sagging. "We will what, Lucas?"

THAT NIGHT TURNED cold, a brush tipped with frost flicking over the wilderness. Daniel sat alone on the porch in Momma's chair and watched the moon cast shadows across the trees. Night birds and frogs sounded, calling and answering each other. *Their songs must be what music is like*, he thought. Momma used to sing when she was healthy, but she told him there were also man-made instruments which could produce song. She used to dance and sing and make music with others, long before the townspeople settled the land.

The townspeople were out there, somewhere, and Daniel narrowed his eyes as he looked carefully at each shadow in the surrounding woods.

"It's funny, I've never even seen a townsperson before," he said. "Momma says to stay away from them, but I don't even know who *they* are."

A cicada rested on his shoulder. It chirped into Daniel's ear, sounding like raindrops batting on the tin roof.

Daniel replied, "I *know* they must look like the rest of us, but I wouldn't care to meet them, seein' as what happened to Poppa."

The cicada extended its wings and chirped again.

"That ain't true about Poppa and you know it," Daniel said. "Momma says he was murdered and this world is a cruel, cruel place."

The cicada climbed over his shoulder and ascended his neck.

"Quit it, Ezekiel. I've told you before that tickles me."

It flew off and circled around to perch on Daniel's outstretched hand.

"Momma's real sick, now. I don't think she's going to live through the week. I'm going to be the last of the family...I'll be all alone."

The cicada rubbed its antennae and chirped to Daniel in a series of rising tones.

"Thanks. That's not what I meant. I know you and the others will still be here."

"DANIEL," MOMMA CRIED out.

"Coming," he said.

Daniel was in the kitchen brewing her morning tea. He shuffled to her room, a small space separated from the main parlor by a faded sheet filled with red-and-gold images of mythical animals that stood upright in tunics. He sometimes wondered if Momma were as old as the images on that fabric.

Behind the sheet she lay in bed, staring at him, her eyes open wide and aware. A spiral of blood and snot hung from her nose, and drops splattered on her nightgown. She spoke in a voice which sounded clear and strong. "I'm dying."

"I know," he replied. He felt honest at saying those words out loud. He understood she'd been dying for a long time, but they lived their life together as they always had, without ever speaking of it.

"I haven't much time," she said. "My mind plays tricks on me, little pranks I once would have laughed away as a child. Now though, I don't know what's real, or dream, or memory. I've been asleep for so long…"

Daniel gently handed her the cup of tea and kept his hand placed over her own as she drank.

"I had a dream, Daniel. A vision of the holy land." She coughed, then wheezed, and Daniel could hear the death-rattle, like pebbles grating in her lungs. "Your Poppa was there, waiting for me. He said he's happy, but it's lonely without us. There's a place set for me at the golden table, and all my sins and black transgressions will be forgiven if only I undo the evil I have wrought."

"You and Poppa back together?" Daniel squeezed her shoulder and his eyes widened. He only knew Poppa from her stories and the sad oil painting that hung crooked in the parlor.

"But first I've got to free the spirits of the townspeople I've bound to this land."

"You're going to let them go?" Daniel asked. She once told him that she kept their souls trapped in the woods like moths in a jar. He had asked what that meant, but she never chewed over details. *Knowing too much leads to wicked ideas*, Momma had told him.

He continued. "But all my life you said there's nothing more important than revenge on Poppa's killers. We still ain't ever found what happened to him."

"There's no peace found by keeping a grudge," she said. "I realize that now. The townspeople know I'm dying...I hear their whispers in the wind. They hate me, and they're waiting..."

"How could anyone hate *you*, Momma?"

"I cursed them...all of them. I cursed the earth like an ulcer, oozing cancer to rot the town. I wouldn't let the ulcer heal, and it spread. I cursed everyone, so they'd die and their spirits could never find rest 'til I found what happened to your Poppa. It was a curse that took everything out of me and made me sick." She turned and buried her face in the pillow. She spoke again, and her muffled voice broke in a sob. "I filled myself with black magic, more than I ever had before, and it poisoned me. You were inside of me still, and it poisoned you too. That's why you don't look like your brothers."

Daniel felt a sharp sting, as if the flying bugs from the marsh crept inside and bit his heart.

"We've got to leave this dead land in our own ways. I'm sorry—real sorry—I've held you back. I've kept you hidden from the world, 'cause of my fears, my hate of the townspeople." Momma turned back and her face was wet. Blood smeared her lips. "Lord, my poor, poor boys. Your brothers weren't meant to suffer, but the curse didn't discriminate. It seized them like the others...I thought I could control it."

"But they ain't suffering. They're all around us," he said.

Her face crinkled like a dried flower and confusion washed over her eyes. She opened her mouth to speak and stayed like that, in silent pause, before responding. "I've done wrong. I've got to free them, if it's not too late already."

"I love you, Momma," Daniel said. "I don't want you to leave."

She shook her head, as if clearing cobwebs off her thoughts. "It's time for us to move on. Your brothers and me...we'll all be a family again up in heaven. All we have to do is get there."

"But this *is* heaven, Momma. We can all stay here."

"Honey, this world is a cruel, cruel place. Nothing is as it seems."

"No," Daniel said suddenly. "I'll be all alone. You can't take them with you."

Her eyes turned oil-black in rage, a flash like colorless lightning. "Boy, you do as I say!"

Just as quickly, the black dissipated and her face fell slack, the weight of her anguish dispersing with the rage. "I need to make one last spell...to release them. You must gather things for me, roots and spiders and water hemlock—I'll tell you a list. You understand...Lucas?"

DANIEL WALKED THROUGH the woods pushing aside Spanish moss and batting at mosquitoes and snakeflies that hovered with each step. He carried a wicker basket yellow as a summer daffodil and, as he hobbled over wet ground, he placed things inside.

"Ezekiel, why don't you talk to Momma like you talk to me?" Daniel said. He'd asked that question to each of his brothers many times, never satisfied with their lack of explanation. "It's never made sense I can hear you just fine, but she can't."

The cicada hovered in the air, wings buzzing close to Daniel's face. Ezekiel spoke in a series of clicks and peeps like the warble of a whippoorwill.

"Momma doesn't believe you're with us. She thinks everyone's trapped in some limbo, like ghosts walking the land."

Ezekiel chirped and settled on Daniel's disfigured shoulder.

"But how can you be a ghost if you're a critter?" Daniel asked. "You got flesh and blood like me. Even though we look different on the outside, you and me is the same on the inside, just like Momma always told us growing up."

Ezekiel chirped again, its tone rising like a brewing storm.

"All of Momma's children living around her and she don't even know. She wants to make a spell to kill everyone and take you to heaven with her," Daniel said.

He stopped under a black cypress that leaned to the earth, burdened by half-dead limbs and clumps of beryl lichen. He peeled off lichen by the handful and set it inside the basket, held in the crook of his limp arm. Ezekiel jumped into the air and started to speak, but Daniel interrupted.

"It's murder, and murder's bad, just like what happened to Poppa. Momma's so confused now, she don't know what she's saying."

Ezekiel flew to face Daniel and they stared deep into each other's eyes, searching tenuous boundaries to find compromise. The cicada clicked rapidly, telling old stories from the shadows of perpetual dusk.

Daniel listened and nodded when he agreed, and shook his head when he didn't. They were silent awhile, and he moved onwards, deeper into the marsh, gathering lilac root and hideous spotted beetles, fleshy mushrooms and poisonous crabapple fruits from manchineels. The further he travelled from home, the colder the air turned, as if he sank slowly through a river into the deeps that sunlight could not reach.

Ezekiel hopped to a branch and raked its legs through hanging ivy. Daniel turned, alone, to see the purple-striped blooms of water hemlock growing next to its look-alike kin, the parsnip plant. One was harmless, if not edible, and the other a slow death. When he was a boy, and Momma could still walk, she showed him the woods' great mysteries and taught him the secrets of the plants. Once she caught him about to pop a leaf of hemlock into his mouth and slapped it from him so hard he thought her hands were made of mountain.

In appearance, the two were nearly identical, and he thought she wouldn't notice the difference now in her fugue state. He plucked a sprig of parsnip, and Ezekiel saw him.

By the time he returned home, the sun sagged behind a lattice-work of cypresses that surrounded Daniel's home. Things he picked nestled and crawled in the wicker basket, and Ezekiel sat on his shoulder chirping rapidly, its series of clicks sounding like a lecture that was half admonishment and half plea.

"My mind is made up, and it don't matter what you say," Daniel muttered. "I won't let her take y'all away."

He reached the porch, ascended its rickety stairs, and walked through the kitchen into Momma's room.

"I'm back," he said. "I gathered what you needed."

Momma lay stiff in bed with her mouth hinged open. A bramble fly dipped down into her gullet and flew back out, its wings buzzing across cold lips.

"Momma, no—" Daniel fell to her side and a weight of loneliness and remorse sank upon him. He suddenly didn't care if she was half out of her mind, or if he had to fetch her tea five times a day, or oblige any of her strange whims. He just wanted to hold her body and feel her hold him back. He wanted to tell her again that he loved her.

Ezekiel leapt off Daniel and chased away the bramble fly.

Daniel knelt by Momma's bedside and caressed her face, wondering how many times she had done the same to him? He remembered as a boy, lying on a plank bed with each of his brothers curled around him, and Momma stroking his cheek, whispering that he was beautiful and would one day be stronger than them all. He wished more than anything for that moment with her to last forever.

He heard a quick clatter from the porch, as if spindly legs ran across the weather-beaten boards and then darted off.

"They're coming already, ain't they?" Daniel asked. "The townspeople are here, just like she said."

Ezekiel clicked and flew out the room.

Daniel squeezed her hand. It was cold, and he felt strange to hold the limp weight. He gently rolled down the lids over her empty, white eyes.

The clattering steps from the porch grew louder and spread into the parlor, accompanied by the loud buzz of a thousand wings. It sounded like a nest of rattlesnakes in dry grass.

Ezekiel flew back into the room, followed by their five brothers, colored orange and copper and mint-green. The cicadas lined up in order of age next to Momma on the bedside.

Daniel kissed her and stood up. He spoke as if in eulogy. "It's better this way. You thought you cursed the land but, the way I figure, you've blessed us to stay together. We'll never die forever."

Swarms of cicadas began to pour into the room, jostling between the sides of the sheet and doorway. There was a smell to them that Daniel had never noticed when around only a few at a time. But, in mass, he was struck by their musty odor, like old moth balls left for too long in a sealed closet. Their droning wings filled the air with a wild clatter, and he almost had to cover his ears as they flew to Momma, covering her body with their terrible roar. Soon, she could not be seen at all and, instead, there appeared only a mountain of writhing insects, fluttering and spitting out syrupy secretion from their quivering proboscises.

Daniel's brothers joined them.

Daniel had never seen the transformation before—Lucas tried explaining it to him one evening, but it was a thing which Daniel could not understand. The closest he imagined was a butterfly emerging from the cocoon it cast, but that was only similar in terms of the physical impression, rather than the physiological process. He watched the cicadas climb over her and over each other, emitting sticky residue like golden honeycomb. Soon, Momma was immersed in the secretion. It hardened and cracked, as mud does under the sun, until she looked like a great rigid pod, the features of her bones pressing up from beneath.

Moving as one, the insects rose from her in a dark, glittering cloud and flew from the room. As they left, the cicadas introduced themselves to Daniel, those long-ago townspeople he had never before met.

It was true, they told him, that they once hated Momma. But her curse caused their rebirth, and they cherished her as a herald of immortality. She was the mother of them all.

MOMMA'S SHELL LAY in bed for several days, a frozen monument to her majesty. Her remains mummified, turning to a rigid, brown mask of hard lines, so unlike the soft flesh that once dimpled with each smile and laugh. Daniel sat with her, stroking the calcified husk and talking to her as he did all his life.

"Orlie says he sure misses your singing. I reckon I do, too."

He traced one finger along a hollow knot that he thought might have been her mouth.

"Your voice was beautiful, Momma."

A wind blew through the trees, sounding like distant murmurs. The house creaked on its foundation.

Daniel cupped one hand under his cheek and leaned in closer. "I wish I knew Poppa. Ezekiel says he wasn't killed at all, just ran off one day with sights set on a new life. I don't know why Ezekiel says that; wouldn't nobody abandon *you*, Momma.

"You were so powerful. You bound the souls of the towns-people to this land so they couldn't leave. But the thing is, they don't want to leave. They say Poppa's trying to trick you and there ain't nothing after death but lonely cold shadows. It's a good life to remain, when your friends and family are still around. That's why I'll never leave you. We all love you, even the townspeople. They just want to keep you right here with them."

The shell quivered.

Daniel ran his finger down the ridges of her neck to the pitted hollow of her chest. Between the bulging remnants of weary breasts, a thin crack split.

"Don't be scared. C'mon out," he said.

The split widened like a yawning mouth and a pair of pale green legs poked out. A mass pushed from underneath the shell and the chest broke open as if poking up through a piece of wet paper. A cicada emerged, glistening and trembling.

"I'm sorry, Momma. I'm real sorry. I was gonna fix it so your spell didn't work."

He extended his open hand to the crumbling husk. The cicada climbed up his middle finger, probing tentatively with bobbing feelers. Daniel carried it to the parlor and set it on the kitchen table. Poppa's portrait faced them.

"But you see, we're all here, we're a family again. Here comes

Aaron and Lucas, and there's Henry and Ezekiel and Orlie and William."

Six cicadas flew to the table top, landing with taps and chirps.

"You said this world is a cruel, cruel place, and maybe you're right. Maybe you're right, too, about Poppa at the golden table. But maybe the townspeople are right. Nothing is as it seems. I remember your list, Momma, and maybe one day, when I'm tired and can't go on no more, I'll go out and pick the right ingredients."

The cicadas circled her.

"But for now, I think you'll be happy. Like you always said, *heaven is family*."

He leaned down and whispered into her ear. "I love you, Momma."

Each of her other sons repeated the sentiment, and six more times were said, *I love you, Momma*.

THE TREES ARE TALL HERE

Marc E. Fitch

———◆———

THE TREES ARE tall here, in this new place that I have come. And at night I hear them moving. Not just their branches and leaves swaying in the breeze, but rather I hear them encroaching, gathering around us, darkening the world and blotting out the moon. On the surface nothing appears different, except that, maybe, weeks ago I could see through small gaps in the forest to another farmhouse in the distance or patches of blue summer sky. But no longer. The small gaps of light and breadth have disappeared and are now only leaves flickering pale green and back to black.

A tall man with long hair came to our house. He had no car and must have walked the endless straight road that cut through the tobacco fields. He asked my name and I told him. He said he was an artist and he wanted to paint the landscape. He had the eyes of a crow, they twitched and darted, noting small things, tiny things that lit on the breeze that no human should notice. My father came to the door suspicious and probably already beginning to clench his fist. The man said if he could paint here he would give us the paintings to hang in the house. "It's considered good luck to have a painting of your property," he said. My father looked at him with hard, angry eyes. I begged him to let the man paint our house. It would be nice to have someone else here instead of being alone all the time. My father agreed. He said that he would paint something special just for me.

It was only a small farm and the front was the tobacco fields and in the back was the black and terrifying woods. My father didn't notice. He worked too hard in the field tending to the rows of tobacco that raced like a little boy running along the road, each row a leg, the head disappearing into the thick trees. He said we could live on one hundred acres, just me and him. Mom and Thomas were dead now, buried in a patch of land at the farthest corner of our plot beneath a weeping willow that cried at night.

Moss hung from branches, dripping with decay.

I watched my father tend to the field of leafy undergrowth that had been dried and smoked for millennia. I watched the artist set up his easel in the dusk, dressed in black and sweating from the southern humidity. I watched him as he stared past our farmhouse and out into the woods where the trees were tall and moved at night.

I tended the chickens that stopped giving eggs and I milked the cows that had gone dry from spooked nerves. Father's harvester was on the fritz and things were looking bad. Dad got drunk one night and said that small farmers don't stand a chance these days but the next morning he was back out working on the harvester and calling the veterinarian to see what was wrong with our chickens and cows.

I put my hair in braids and took our specially packed tobacco to the farmers' market where college students liked to buy it and make boyish eyes and perverted comments to me. They rolled their own cigarettes and felt at one with the land and talked about Native Americans and everything we had stolen from them. They wore wool caps in the heat and tight black jeans and asked me when we would start growing marijuana. I smiled and said nothing back. "Farmers' daughters really are cute," one of them said. He was always there every Friday at the market and he always looked at me with this sly smile that told me he was dangerous.

I sold almost all of our bags of tobacco and then traded with Harley and Mona for eggs and milk.

"What's wrong with your stock?" Harley said. It was pride masked as concern that farmers use when they see others struggling; it somehow makes them feel superior to be producing when others are struggling.

"Don't know. Something seems to have spooked them."

"There's been talk of a big cat in the area," Harley said. "Took a go at a horse a couple miles away. Tell your dad to keep an eye out and you keep an eye out, too. Little girl like you would make a tasty snack for one of those things."

"I will," I said. But I knew it wasn't a big cat. I knew it was nothing that simple or easy. It was the slow and steady pressure of the forest with the tall trees that moved at night.

The artist was back when I got home. He had his easel set up and was painting and he kept looking out at the trees and then returning to his work. I walked up behind him and spied on his painting.

"Why are you painting something that ain't there?" I said.

"It is there," he said. "Just not in the way we are accustomed to."

The painting was of a massive birch tree with the farmhouse and forest in the background. I remembered the tree. In the background the forest was a deep, dark blackness that seemed to form a face of some kind.

"That tree came down last year. It was hit by lightning," I said. "It was tall."

"It was tall and old," he repeated.

"So why do you paint it?"

"I paint what I see. You don't see it, but I still do. It is still there in another time and place."

"Why does the forest look so scary?"

"Because the birch is gone now and the forest can overtake

anything it sets its mind to."

"How many paintings are you making?"

"Three," he said. "It's a sequence."

"You know Indians used to live here?" I said.

That night there was something else in the trees, something large, roaming through the underbrush, seizing and sending birds and bats into the sky. It smelled of wet earth and ground-up milkweed. I could almost see it there beneath the light of the moon as it stalked among the tall trees. I suddenly heard an ear-shattering gun-shot from just outside my window and I saw that flash of yellow fire like lightening. Then another. Then another. I went to my window and looked down. My father was on the back porch with his rifle firing shots into the trees, pulling back on the bolt, loading another round of .30-06 and firing again. Not even taking the time to aim. His motions jerky and panicked, not smooth like a hunter, but like a cornered animal.

"Harley says there's a cougar around and it might be what's spooking the cows and chickens," I said but Dad was silent. It was bright morning, dry, pale and hot and he was just staring out the window of our kitchen, out into the trees, dead silent with his coffee in hand.

"What were you shooting at last night?" I asked.

"Just target shooting," he said.

"At night?"

He looked at me, clearly annoyed. "When else do you think cougars come stalking around?"

In the afternoon he was able to get the harvester fixed and was out working the rows. I hated the harvester, its three wheels, glass eyes of its cabin, insectoid arms and diesel fumes made it seem like some kind of bright red monster shuffling up and down the furrows gobbling everything, consuming, no matter who or what was in front of it. The clouds were building at the horizon, dark and ominous and there was a wind that was pushing against the leaves and turning their pale underbellies skyward. I walked out to the willow where my mother and brother were buried. I sat down next to the two crosses that served as headstones and let the moss and pollen fall in my hair.

Then the artist was there with me and he said, "What happened to them?"

I didn't answer. Instead, I said, "Are you putting them in your painting?"

"I see them, so I will."

I watched my father in the harvester, churning and chugging, and the clouds purling at the borderland. Then I turned and looked into the forest where it was dark and cool and so unbelievably thick. The tall trees looked like revival worshipers with their hands raised to God in holy ecstasy rocking back and forth in the coming storm.

"They was killed," I said. "There was a man. The police say he killed a lot of people. He came here preaching the good Word with Bibles for sale. Me and daddy were away at the market. Momma and Thomas were here. He used a knife. Daddy never told me what happened but we weren't allowed to see their faces at the wake. Everyone cried and hugged me. I hated it."

The artist looked into my eyes and I could tell that he was good and gentle. "The world is a terrible place," he said. He pulled me close and kissed me once on the forehead and then went back to his easel.

The storm came and the rain pounded against the windows and roof like gravel thrown by a lynch mob. Lightning danced across the fields. Everything was electric. I watched out the window. There were flashes of light and in those flashes I saw things in the woods. I saw the tall trees leaning down and staring at me with strange eyes. But it was like a flipbook cartoon. It was like a memory. I never saw them move, I just saw that they had moved and that was the most frightening part.

And I saw a figure out there in front of the trees, walking behind them, disappearing from view and appearing again. I recognized him as the artist. I pressed my face and hands up to the glass. I saw the trees bending down toward him, embracing him.

The wind whipped against my nightdress and the rain came in waves carried by the gales. I was drenched and the air was cold. There was lightning everywhere and the sound of sirens in my ear. I ran out to the edge of the trees and was calling for him but my voice was lost in wind and rain. My eyes strained but everything was moving, the leaves whipping and turning and the rain pounding the bark and underbrush. The trees were so unbelievably tall here, swaying, bending in the lightning strobe. I looked everywhere but he was gone. I stepped into the underbrush moving beneath the trees, entering into their embrace where the wind was blocked and the rain came in big drops that rolled off the leaves and suddenly everything seemed calm and quiet and I stared into the dark recess of the trees and saw a pair of eyes staring back at me, bright yellow and predatory in the night. They watched me with a cunning stillness and I stopped in my tracks. It was not the artist. The lightning flashed and lit up the whole world and I saw it there, crouched in the leaves, spine coiled like a spring, fat, padded paws tense on the wet earth, ears pulled back against its dreaded triangular head. It tensed and then sprang and I was running toward my house, the dim porch light the only sign of life left in the world.

The cougar padded softly and swiftly. I could feel it almost on me, my voice hoarse, sucking in rainwater enough to drown. It swiped at my ankle and I felt a dagger pierce my skin and my calf muscle shuttered in electric shock. The second swipe knocked my foot out from underneath me and then I was in the grass, the water rising up on me, and there was the feeling of hot, wet fur and carrion breath at my neck and then a thunderclap that sent vibrations reeling through my skull. All I could feel then was warmth.

My father was there, standing over me, rifle in hand. He towered over me like the tall trees of the night and he let off another shot at the ground near to me. Then he picked me up and I was galloping into the light, the only life left in the world.

WORD GOT AROUND about the cougar attack and Father dragged

its carcass by the scruff of the neck and skinned it in the barn. I got stitches in my calf and shots to ward off the infection. Everyone at the farmers' market asked how I was feeling and examined the bandaging. I recounted the story a dozen times and I sold more tobacco than I ever had before. "What were you doing out there in that storm?" Harley asked, but I couldn't give him an answer that made any sense. None of it made sense to me, so I told them that I had been sleepwalking. Maybe that was true.

The college student that was always staring at me made a comment about the loss of such a beautiful creature. "Too bad it had to die," he said. I punched him in the face and Harley sent him scrambling and whimpering to his friends.

When I came home, my father was once again in the field with the harvester and the day was bright and dry and warm. I walked into our house and there was something different. It felt safer somehow, more secure and stronger than it ever had before. I walked through the place like a ghost, touching nothing, disturbing nothing, drawn to the living room like moth to flame.

There, above the fireplace, was the painting of the big birch tree and the farmhouse and the monstrous woods in the background. It was framed in wood and hung above the mantle. I walked over and stared at it. It wasn't the greatest thing I had ever seen, it wasn't perfect. The images were disjointed, just slightly off-kilter and out of focus. I looked closer and closer and deep in the black hues of the woods I saw something very faint, very light, too tiny to be truly seen.

My father appeared in the doorway. "He dropped this and two others off this morning. Said he's all finished here. Kinda weird, if you ask me," he said.

"Yes," I said.

"There's another in the kitchen and one hung up in your room," he said.

I walked to the kitchen and saw the second of the sequence hung above the kitchen table. It was the same disjointed image but magnified one hundred times so that the trees nearly covered the canvas and Mother and Thomas' crosses could be seen in the very far corner. But the slight, ghostly figure in the trees was so much more visible with its light brush strokes against the raging blackness; a girl in a night dress, soaked to the skin, rain dripping from beyond the borders. Now, I could truly see the frightening darkness of the trees that moved in the night and I could see the faint figure. My eyes and mind magnified the image like a fever dream and maybe that is what it was, the infection from the cat claws reaching into my brain.

I ran upstairs. It was there above my bed in a gilded frame this time, something cheap but with the appearance of gold. This painting was different. The darkness of the tall trees engulfed the work but there in the middle was the ghostly figure in a night-dress. It was me on that night, soaked, facing into the woods, into the maw of the cavernous trees, whose branches were reaching down through the storm, a small light from our farmhouse in the background. It was an image painted from the perspective of the forest, as if he had been there that night, looking out at me from the darkness, furiously working at his easel. I could see myself in my nightdress, just beyond the shadows, with dark branches reaching over me and my face in a fearful, ghastly scream.

I rushed out of the house and ran down the driveway in the hot, dry sun with the smell of cut tobacco.

I stood in the dusty road that stretched for miles into the horizon with the lost boy running in the rows and furrows of tobacco farms and I called for him again and again. My father watched me from the doorway and I could tell that he was terrified of having a daughter, of having a last piece of himself that he could lose forever; a piece of himself that he couldn't understand anymore without his wife and son to help him.

He said that he saw things that were not there.

He said the world is a terrible place.

My face was an expression of slowly dawning terror, staring into the darkness and the artist staring back out at me.

A Quiet Axe

Michael Kelly

———◆———

FLAT LANDS. CRACKED. Heaving. The earth a dry grey tongue. Ghost wisps in the ancient, unsmiling sky. Something finally floating free. A dead thing.

A shack, wind-worn and blanched, boards warped, the wind through the wood singing of madness, like the snap of old bone. Gutters droop under a weighty existence, frowning.

Inside, a man and a woman. He was quick to violence was the man, like a sudden tornado, black and twisted. He'd beat her, and she'd fall, but she couldn't leave. There was nowhere to go. Nothing for miles around but the arid dry land and dusty sky, both ceaseless and unending like her life.

She would think of Becca sometimes, and she'd cry. She couldn't keep it in, not like the man. She'd never seen him cry. He was stoic, dry-eyed, even as his fists preached to her. She wondered if he cried on the inside, if a veil of tears exploded inside his head with each fist-fall, coating his dark skull in a curtain of warm remorse or cold pity. Too much a man to show it. Even that time in the barn, when he was finished with the stray she'd been feed-

131

ing, he wore a face of smooth stone, as cold and quiet as the axe in his hand. Hers' though…hers' was a face of sorrows, rutted like the forsaken earth.

Him. Everything inside, bottled up. Nothing leaking out. He'd blamed her, and the land. *Your fault*, he'd said. *Ain't got no call for feeding strays, making them dependent. Can barely feed ourselves. Too many mouths.* Face impassive, his body taut and still as a Cobra's before a strike. *The land is a dead thing.* Shaking now. *A dead thing.*

The woman wondered if the man ever thought about Becca. Wondered if he'd ever given her more than a passing thought, or if, in his eyes, she was just another stray. Thoughts of Becca were the only things keeping the woman tethered to this lifeless land. Like the dead, she yearned to be moor-less.

She glanced to the floor, at the man. There was nothing inside him, really, after all. Not anymore. Just a spreading dark wetness, seeping through the floor into the parched and greedy earth.

Outside, the weary sky frowned and the wind murmured of lunacy, like a quiet axe.

Inside, the man gazed upward, dry-eyed and unblinking. The woman dried her hands in the folds of her dress and squinted through a dirt-smeared window at a barren world. She trembled, blinked, but didn't weep. Not this time. She kept it inside, and it made her buoyant. After a time she went outside and floated away, a ghost of herself.

THE DEATH OF YATAGARASU

Bethany W. Pope

————◆————

CROW TURNS TO face the first bluish light of dawn. His right eye stopped working some time ago; the last time he caught sight of himself (in the freshly-polished hubcap of a brand-new Mercedes) his reflection through that eye was very blurred—something milky-white was growing across the iris; an infection that he could not name. Possibly, it is a side-effect of aging. All of his nest-mates died winters ago; young enough so that their feathers were all in place, black, with a healthy green gloss. Now, the eye is totally blind.

Crow considers himself peerless. He clacks his beak, scratches his scabrous leg.

This morning is not particularly cool. The year is ripe and food is plentiful outside the fence. Still, his bones hurt, his joints. The last time he molted his feathers grew back patchy; his pinions swivel loose in their sockets and his pink skin shows. He rarely flies now; when he does he is clumsy. It is better to hop, much more energy efficient. Soaring is wonderful, he thinks, once you get up to where the thermals can carry you. But the climb is exhausting.

His wings are too weak to bear the burden of his bulk.

Crow's left eye has also become unreliable. He bashes a wing on a tire as he exits the cave he found beneath the low maroon body of the latest model. It is one of thirty on the lot. He has his choice of nest-sites, even now that the trees are forbidden him.

He has no competition.

The razor-wire fence keeps out the cats and the guard dogs are well-fed; they do not bother him. The night watchman, a fat, lank-haired man who was probably born the same year Crow hatched, has never noticed him. The last time Crow saw him, the man was sitting on the front bumper of a lapis-blue model, sinking the chassis beneath the weight of his flabby blue-clad behind. He was chewing a Snickers bar and staring vacantly into the jaundiced light of a sodium arc lamp. Crow thinks, secretly, that the guard isn't very bright—not that this stops him from feasting on the fat man's leftovers.

Crow has been living in this vast expanse of rubber and metal since before the first frost. When the snow fell he was sheltered by cars. The lot was regularly shoveled. Life here is easy. There aren't any predators. In the daytime men and women wander around in suits, staring at clip-boards, small glowing oblongs, and gabbling in their strange liquid tongue at the occasional customer, but if he remains silent, if he resists the urge to call, they rarely bother him. Food is not abundant, limited to fast-food scraps and the occasional lost insect, but he never has to fight for it. Every share is his.

He survived the winter.

If he had remained in the park, he would not have done so. He has become too slow. A cat would catch and make a meal of him. One of those roving bands of adolescent male rooks would find him and finish what the last group started; it took months for his wing to heal from that last attack. They came on him in a group, their black eyes hungry, their voices raw. He still bears a long and ragged scar (it stands naked and pink, a lightning-line running down from his left shoulder) left over from his last encounter with the barely-fledged juveniles who would have torn the flesh from his bones.

Remembering the pain, he thinks, I would have been gamey, but protein is protein. In his heart, Crow does not blame them. He would have done the same, when he was young.

As it was, he kicked, he fought, he pecked and scratched as hard as he could. Crow barely escaped them and his recovery was slow. He couldn't do so now.

Yes, he is safe here. Comfortable. He doesn't know why it isn't enough.

Each night, he huddles down, fluffing his remaining feathers to trap his fleeting warmth. He closes his eyes (the quick and the dead) and up he goes into a sunset the same wonderful color as a mouse's insides. He soars on thermals that flow like a blood-river, carrying his strong body across a landscape the shade of a ripening bruise. Flight is a dream the dawn shatters, and each dawn here is cold and gray. He is so tired of having a full belly and an empty heart.

Crow wants out.

He drags himself through rows of vehicles (stiff as rigor mortis) to the dumpster behind the low-slung boxy main building. This is where the deals are made, where papers are signed, handshakes exchanged, and meals eaten. The dumpster is full and a white box (insides coated with something sweet and lurid orange) has spilled onto the ground. He allows himself a happy grunt. He will not have to climb the metal box to plunder the top of the pile. He can conserve his energy for something greater.

Crow eats.

He scrapes citrus-tinted syrup (vaguely flavored with meat, slightly tainted with paper) into his obsidian bill. If he strains with his good eye he can see the contrast he makes with the colors and he is flushed with pleasure at the sight of it. His razor-sharp beak is his one undulled, unfaded feature. This syrup makes him feel young. It's the high-sugar content. It's the resemblance to dried blood.

Fed, his body tricked to youth for a few minutes and the sun rising brighter every minute, he hops as fast as he can to the fence that divides the car lot from a small city park. The fence is ten feet tall and topped with loops of slicing wire. The park itself is overgrown and filth-littered. He can smell cat from here. The shrubs are poisoned with the urine of dogs. He can smell mice. There are nettles underneath all of the bushes and not a leaf of soothing burdock to be seen; it is all so vibrantly alive. He knows that it will kill him.

Crow doesn't care.

Crow hooks his beak into the lower corner of a chain-link diamond; he uses the strength of his last tool to haul his ragged body up. Weakly, he grips the links on either side of his head with his feet. He rests a moment, then reaches up to grasp another diamond. The climb is slow, and painful. The sun is quite high when he reaches the top.

There is a gap between the top of the fence and the loops of brownish razor-wire that threaten to shave off his plumage at the cuticle. Ducking, he wedges himself beneath the blades. His back hurts, but he won't have to endure it for long. He takes in this view, the patchy, yellowed grass, the weeds, the garbage. It is the last and richest visage of his life. Crow stretches out his neck and delivers three caws. They are as loud, as ugly and joyful as any love-struck crow-song.

Crow swallows. Coughs.

Crow spreads his wings.

Crow soars.

THE COOING

John Claude Smith

———◆———

"CREEPY, EH?" MAGDALENE heard a slight clinking sound, not unlike glasses of champagne kissing on New Year's Eve, as the warm wind delicately rattled the jagged shards of glass jutting out of the broken window pane in the abandoned house her girl-friend, Samantha, and she were exploring. Despite the heat, she wrapped her arms around herself a little tighter.

Middle of the summer, it was so far from New Year's Eve. Out here, it seemed so far away from everything.

"Beautiful," Sam said, clicking off picture after picture, enamored by their inspiring find: a splintered door frame; a toppled, torn sofa; a gaping hole in the hallway wall; and other signifiers of disrepair and forgotten dreams. On and on, she was in her pre-ferred version of Heaven.

Empty Houses was her new project. This abandoned farmhouse with its ravaged soul on full display, a dozen miles down the road from an equally depressing and discarded town, fascinated her deeply. She lived for desolation in all its spirit-draining glory.

Magdalene went along for the ride, her fascination geared toward Sam. The things one did for love.

Three other cars were parked along the dirt road across from the house. The desert stretched out beyond the vehicles, a pale sheen burning off the surface as the sun swelled with an intensity they had rarely ever experienced. The temperature settled between a hungry, flesh-singeing crematorium, and Hell. When walking past the other cars, Magdalene ran a slim finger across two of them, the dust thick and sticking, despite the hot breeze. It seemed to her the breeze did not blow any of it away, instead pressing it into the painted skin. The third car seemed more recent, but signs of any of the inhabitants were nowhere to be seen. They were probably already inside. Fellow explorers, lost in the wooden carcass.

"Oh," she said, startled by a cooing sound from somewhere outside. She'd spotted a few hawks lazily gliding across the fading blue into bone white sky on their way here, but this sound could not be one of theirs. A pigeon? A turtledove? She had no idea, but did not expect either of those birds were indigenous to the southwest. But what did she know?

All she knew for sure was the silence in places like this made her ears ache. The cooing of a pigeon or some similarly inclined to sing bird shattered the silence in an unpleasant way.

"Just a pigeon, honey. No reason to get all jumpy."

She wondered if it really *was* a pigeon, if pigeons haunted dreary places like this. Perhaps it was a Raven, Poe's Raven, come to wish her a miserable day.

Sam strolled into another room, sandals clapping at her progress, getting lost in her art, her obsessive ways. Magdalene followed dutifully behind, a stray puppy in need of attention.

Again, the cooing rattled her spine. Something was amiss about it that made her dig her fingernails into her palms.

"Sounds hoarse," she said, more to break her escalating anxiety than in expecting a response, verbally dusting the bird away.

"A horse? What are you talking about? It's obviously a bird."

"No." She sighed under her breath.

Sam canted her head toward Magdalene, catching the sigh in her ears and registering Magdalene's annoyance, along with her always brittle mood.

"The cooing sound, it's hoarse. Rough. Very un-bird-like."

"Dry up here. Perhaps the bird's sick or thirsty. Why don't you head out to the car and give it some of your water?"

Magdalene sensed the exasperated tone propping up Sam's words, ignored them, and entered the room behind her—a kitchen. Sam was smitten by dishes left dirty for eternity in a cluttered sink. The whirr and click of Sam's camera was almost soothing, when the cooing ratcheted up a notch. Insistent and, like her, in need of attention.

Sam ignored her, knowing any further conversation would only lead to the petty arguments that littered their relationship. Now was not the time for one. Never was the time for one...

Magdalene shuffled her feet, hands buried in her denim pockets, watching Sam in her khaki shorts as she worked, wishing she had worn something that let her skin breathe and wanting away from this sad place. Why Sam found places like this interesting made no sense to her. Magdalene found darkness and melancholy in words appealing, her gothic heart smitten by those who wielded words in such a way, almost romantic. But not in real life, where such designs left her uneasy. Where's the beauty here, despite Sam's statement earlier that it was beautiful? Somebody, a family, had dreamed here, grew up here. Perhaps died here. Left it as barren as her heart often felt when she watched how Sam fully immersed herself in the foreboding vacancy of places like this. But places like this, where the dead landscape outside—cactus flourished, but the land was brown and riddled with weeds—drew Sam's focus in a way Magdalene never felt she would, simply made her unhappy. Even jealous.

A stunted scream cut through the cooing, as well as Sam's concentration.

"The hell was that?"

"A reason to leave," Magdalene said, pulling on Sam's arm as goosebumps frolicked along hers. Sam gently, firmly peeled herself from Magdalene's grasp, ears perked up as a cat's and said, "So abrupt. Probably one of the people from the cars out front just stubbed a toe. Or found a nest of spiders." She laughed, but there was no humor in it. She yelled out, "Hey, you all right?" to the silence, where it hung unattended for a smattering of seconds before the cooing recommenced.

"There. See. It didn't even scare off the bird, why should it scare us off?" She smiled at Magdalene, but, again, there was no joy in it. A false face for a false statement.

Magdalene knew Sam was feigning courage as she often did, all the damn time. But not now, please. Don't put up this act, let's just go.

"The cooing is closer."

"So what?"

"Sounds harsh. Sounds wrong. And it's getting closer." Magdalene felt herself grow dizzy. From the heat or from this place, she wasn't sure. She placed her hand on the kitchen table for balance, then immediately reclaimed it, wiping sticky fingers on her jeans. Sticky from what, she did not know. Dried jam? Spilled wine?

"Give me a break, dear. It's a goddamn bird. That's all. Don't make it something more than it is." Sam's momentary disquiet and faux courage was shoved aside by her irritation in her dear love, Magdalene's, fragile manner. Her always fragile manner.

"It's in the house," Magdalene said, backing away from Sam, her breath constricting in her chest. Tighter, tighter...

"*What is your problem?*" Sam put her free hand to her hip after brushing one of the many loose strands of auburn hair out of her face, miffed to the teeth at Magdalene's over-dramatic ways, not that she should be. The girl lived in a state of perpetual worry.

"It's behind that door," Magdalene said, pointing to the door at the far end of the kitchen. To another room, perhaps a basement; the bird; the cooing.

"It's a fucking pigeon, Maggie. Just a bird. God, I hate how you're always such a scaredy-cat."

The cooing echoed loud off the humid confines of the kitchen. Sam had to admit it was rather discomfiting, but battened down the hatches of her fear and said, "Look. I'm going to open that door and kick the little bastard to Timbuktu. Then I'm going to finish exploring this place while you step outside and do whatever the fuck you need to do to simmer yourself down. Head to the car and read some Keats or Shelley like you always do. Bury yourself in the past."

"No, baby," she said, hurt by the intent of Sam's words, yet more disturbed by the scene playing out to grim completion. "Let's go..."

Magdalene's face was contorted into a mask of dread so complete Sam almost pulled up the camera and took a photo of it.

Magdalene knew when Sam got set in her ways, there was no turning back. She bumped into the wall, not even registering she had been backing out of the room, her instincts set on escape. The entrance was to her left, but she chose to scrunch down against the wall and let this all play out. Let Sam be right again as she kicked the bird to Timbuktu. Nonetheless, she hugged her knees to her damp, Bauhaus' Bela Lugosi's Dead t-shirt, her sweat-soaked breasts.

The cooing was like a suffocating blanket, but Sam ignored her own instincts, instead set on a course for making her point and moving forward.

"Scaredy-cat," she said, a snort of exasperation as she twisted the much colder than she would have expected knob to the door, paint peeling to the damaged wood below—almost as if fingernails had clawed at it, she thought—and swung it open.

"Here birdy-birdy," she said, before the birdy-birdy's wings were clipped by confusion.

The towering figure was adorned with an abundance of feathers stuck to its naked, muscular frame with blood. Barbwire was threaded into the flesh along the sides of its torso and the insides of its arms, indicative of an attempt to make wings; feathers were stuck there as well. Dried, crusted blood coagulated at the intersection of flesh and metal. Fresh blood dripped moistly from its exaggerated leer, accentuating its cockeyed gaze. The leer was set back behind a metal and mesh make-shift beak.

Sam gasped, breath released, surrender at hand. Her legs gave out as she stumbled backwards, landing hard on the wooden chair at the head of the table.

Magdalene started to whimper as a passage from one of her favorite books, Alberto Savinio's *Lives of the Gods*, flashed within the dimming light of her thoughts: "Don't judge me by what you see now; I don't take care of myself, my sufferings have sharpened my beak, and I do nothing but laugh." She pulled her legs even closer, a taut, trembling ball, and tried to make herself smaller. Tried to disappear.

"Coo, coo," it said, a throaty, ugly sound—wrong as Magdalene had suggested; as she had known—as it stepped into the room....

A Knife in My Drawer

Zdravka Evtimova

————◆————

I WAS AFRAID.

Sometimes the sea was quiet and the sun was in the sky all the time, or so I thought. I was tempted to run to the shore and get a swim, but I suspected a storm would break the minute I'd touch the water. That was my imagination of course. I could hear the wind roar and howl and the waves hurled masses of cold rage against the other side of the page. I wrote a short story on the page, but on its other side the ocean growled. The paper was the wall that separated me from the endless freezing water. At times, I asked myself what would happen if I bored a hole in the page, I had even bought a penknife which I kept on my desk. I often forgot what I was writing as I sat there lost, motionless, listening.

"What are you doing?" Len, my husband, asked and I thought I saw fright in his eyes. I didn't tell him about the crags, the surf, the waves hitting against the rocks. I didn't tell him I heard screams of dying birds but he sensed something had gone wrong with me.

"You are unhappy your stories don't sell," he muttered. "Don't be. Stories are nothing. Come here."

When I was with him I couldn't hear the ocean. I was afraid I would miss the rare sunny hours when the waves slept and barely touched the paper on the other side. Those were the prettiest days in my life. I glued my ear to the paper and listened. At first it was only the sigh of rippling water, then sands whispered and the shore was so near I could feel its pebbles on the tips of my fingers.

"You don't speak to our son," Len said. "He needs you. You don't smile at him. You don't notice me."

We had a small house on the shore of the Black Sea. It was Len who bought it. I had never liked the sea. It raged and thundered in winter, in summer tourists infested the shore and the beach was full of them. I turned my back to the waves. Sometimes I swam at night when the beach was a sigh in the air. Then the surf and the night blended and the shore touched the page with the ocean I had left on my desk.

"Maybe I am in love with another woman," Len, my husband, said.

What a funny man he is, I thought. You are free to be in love with anyone you want. You are free but I am not, Len. I want to go behind the page.

"Mother, why don't you write on your computer?" my son asked. "You write nothing on that piece of paper. You are constantly staring at it. There's nothing behind it, Mother."

But I heard slight barely audible tapping on the other side of the page. At first I thought it was a pebble that had hit the paper. Then fear seized me. I thought the sharp edges would cut a hole and my page would be torn into pieces. I panicked: what if the water burst into the house. My son was in his room. My son!

"Do you want me to take you to the other side?" I asked the boy. "There are sunny days there, and the waves are quiet like the pictures on the walls in your room. The water is warm."

"I like the Black Sea more than your page," my son said. "Your page is a lie. You care about an empty piece of paper."

The tapping sound on my page got stronger. I could swear somebody was typing on the other side. The surf was writing a short story for its shore.

The noise stopped abruptly and then the sunniest day behind the page began. I could swear there were seagulls flitting over the surface of the water, the sun shone, and infinity loved me. I reached for the penknife that lay on my desk. I wanted to get there, behind the page.

"I have to go," Len, my husband, said.

"Go," I told him. "You are a free man."

"You used to be so jealous," he breathed. "What's wrong with you?"

"It's what she sees behind the paper," my son said. "The page's changed her."

They'd been gone for a month, my son and my husband, or so I thought. I had not written any stories. I described the sounds the water was making. They were magnificent and powerful. The page was the only barrier that cut me off from my dreams. Maybe Len and my son were at home all the time. Yes, somebody cooked food for me, and I didn't care what had happened to the woman Len was in love with. The tapping sounds on the other side of the paper continued. The ocean was friendly and I thought of the writer on the other side of the page. He was not as tall and handsome as my husband. I believed his face was brown with the sun, and he was tired because he had been writing on the water months on end, and there was no one to read his fairy tales. I felt sorry for him and I tapped the page with a sharp pencil. He answered me. He tapped the paper so carefully, so timidly I could have cried.

"There is no ocean behind the paper and there is no one typing there," my husband who was in love with another woman said. "I want you to be happy the way you were before you found the notebook with a single page in it."

He didn't know these were the loveliest hours redolent of salty water, soothing with the shrieks of seagulls. Was the ocean a string of days I had missed, days that had gone leaving no memory, no trace? Who had settled on the other side of the paper? I lived with my stories in the smallest room, in the unreality of water, on the shore of an angry black sea. I had a husband who was in love with another woman and a son who needed my attention all the time. They were not a part of my happy days. Maybe the shore on the other side of the page was the place where death waited for me, tapping ever so gently on the thin white sheet, letting me know it was much more real than my uneventful life, and the short story I'd printed on the paper was a door to oceans I had never seen. Was it my hope to go there that made a difference? The man, the one who was not very tall and handsome, lived in the story.

He had a long purple scar on his cheek. I like your blue T-shirt, he had said to me. I'll come and find you no matter what. And I'll bring you a blue tulip. There are no blue tulips, the woman who lived in my short story had said. I was that woman. I lived in the words and the paper pulled me out of the stormy waters. I'll bring you a blue tulip, the man repeated and the story ended abruptly. Maybe the biting winds behind the page were my panic I'd never see the tulip. My hopes surged, gleamed then were gone, and I knew they would not come back. My husband's shadow was my home, my room was made of fears, and the waves behind the page hated the night.

"I've torn the page from your notebook," my husband said. "I burned it."

I froze in my tracks. I had no notebook and no ocean. No soothing smell of salt and infinity. I looked at my desk horrified.

"Our son needs you. I need you," my husband said. "I want you to be healthy. There was nothing behind that page. Nothing."

In the evening, I cooked potato soup for them. In the morning, I took my son to the zoo. I hadn't taken him anywhere for months. We ate ice-cream and sandwiches, he told me tales. I listened, I listened hard. The waves were gone. There was no ocean and no seagulls. My son babbled on. My husband brought me flowers and suggested the three of us go to France, to the castles on the Loire, and the French Riviera. I wanted to stay home. I bought a new notebook, and then another one. None of their pages separated me from an ocean of fears and hopes, from squalls and tales of screaming waves. I locked myself in the room and listened. I glued blank pages on the wall and nothing happened. Death and fears had left me, hopes had left me too.

My husband brought me flowers almost every day; my son was happy and cheerful. We invited friends and threw parties. You are beautiful, Anna. You are more beautiful than before. I am so happy you are back, my husband said. He didn't know I kept a sheet of crumpled paper glued to my skin. I prayed to bring the ocean back to me. But the salty wind was gone.

I took a job in the local library. I cooked delicious meals for my family, I took long walks with friends, and I wrote short stories and fairy tales.

"We can go to see the castles on the Loire, what do you think?" my husband said.

I thought I wanted to go.

"I'm glad the yellow rings under your eyes are gone. I'm glad you smile again."

Rarely, at night I heard the waves beat against sharp stones. I heard screams of seagulls, I saw the page again and I wrote on it. The endless water glowed, I wanted to swim to the shore, and I sensed the wind slept in the waves. Very rarely, I heard the tapping sounds and deep in my memories the short story gleamed, pale and silvery, like a shadow of a kite, like a song I had forgotten long ago but it was in the air I breathed.

I was a happy woman again. I had my job and my family. The ocean had vanished and the wind had died. I was free.

On the day before we started for the ancient castles on the Loire, my son and my husband went to buy a new suitcase. I was in the kitchen cooking lunch when the front door bell rang.

"Coming," I called out thinking it was my husband with the new suitcase.

Out of breath, I ran to see it.

A man, not very tall, not very handsome, stood in the door. A long scarlet scar ran down his cheek. I looked at it. I looked at it and could not breathe.

"This is for you," the man said.

He gave me a flower, a tulip.

It was blue. Impossibly blue.

ON BALANCE

Jason A. Wyckoff

———— ♦ ————

PEAK SEASON ENDS with Labor Day, but thriftier tourists continue to rent the beach houses through September. Hurricane season is in full swing by October, and if it is difficult to find lodging then, it is only because some houses are shut for the season and some others are occupied by their actual owners, anxious to enjoy the last of the warm weather as the winds allow.

I preferred this time of year to take my vacation. I did not fish or frolic in the surf, and swam but rarely. I was contented to stroll aimlessly, my slacks rolled to my knees. When I became tired, or found a particularly quiet or attractive spot, I sat in the sand and watched the surf.

On one such occasion, I noticed a man with a metal detector sweeping along the base of the dunes a hundred feet from my repose. Dispel any romantic notions you have of his endeavor— such beach-combers have little expectation of discovering sunken doubloons swept ashore; they troll for lost tourist jewelry. This character struck me as a semi-ambulatory melted waxwork: from his drooping head down through the slack of his faded clothes.

As I watched him shake his tool roughly and then flip the bottom plate to his face with some unknowable inquiry, I felt instinctively his last day on earth would involve the routine cleaning of a firearm. Several times the man stopped to pick something up. Loose change was pocketed; rejected objects were tossed carelessly into the rushes. Just as I lost interest and looked away I heard a particularly loud squeal emanate from his machine. I watched as he set the metal detector aside and used both hands to dig into the sand. He straightened, holding some object I could not see. He peered closely at it and turned it over several times. Then he looked off towards the surf as though weighing a decision of some import. He repeated the process twice more. I was surprised to see him shrug and toss the thing aside indifferently before resuming his hunt.

I attempted to return to my thoughtless ocean vigil, but I found myself distracted. I couldn't help but wonder what sort of thing would cause the treasure-seeker to act in that exact way—what was it that could elicit such intense but ultimately ephemeral interest? I could not guess. And I saw no *reason* to guess, as it couldn't possibly impact me whatever the thing was. Yet my curiosity remained unabated. I waited while he moved further along the beach. When I thought he was far enough away that he would not notice, I went and retrieved the object. It was a small, metal cup, dented in places, most especially on the base opposite the handle. I judged it to be made of tin, but dark, wet sand clung doggedly all over, despite my secondary efforts to wipe it clean, which made it difficult to get a sense of feel. Some luster showed in the polish beneath the earthy patina, and I was surprised the treasure-seeker hadn't added the cup to his haul for further investigation. I noticed some sort of engraving on the cup and rubbed the area vigorously with a thumb. Stippled gothic lettering emerged: *Donna Louise.*

Of course, the name was not known to me. I examined the base to see if there was a maker's mark, but the sand smeared black and would not fall away. Perhaps two minutes passed before

I realized I was duplicating the scavenger's actions exactly—turning the cup over in my hands repeatedly, furrowing my brow in concentration as I peered at it. I even looked away to the horizon as he had, as though it might hold some clue. I realized I was considering the obvious move, which was to rinse the thing in the surf. My deliberation as to whether or not the action was warranted took longer than its accomplishment would have, but I felt frozen, as though the choice would be impossible if I didn't first appreciate the significance of the decision. I am not easily embarrassed, but I suddenly felt foolish when I noticed a boy of about ten watching me. I looked at the cup again but could see no reason it should hold my attention—and that was irksome, for there was no reason it *shouldn't*, for if I chose to be interested by it, then why shouldn't I act as I pleased? There was a grip of mystery upon me that made me hold the cup longer than I might if I didn't care about it, but also anchored me from taking it with me for a laugh, as though the short time invested was sufficient that it could no longer be treated as a lark. Finally, I was exasperated by the very weight of the decision. If I should have been embarrassed about anything, it was my exit: I hurled the thing to the ground and stomped away.

I looked back just before I was to turn up the path over the dune. I saw the boy absorbed in examination, holding the cup near his guileless face.

I VACATIONED ALONG that same stretch of beach the following October, but derived no pleasure from my time there. I returned to work wearier than I left. The next three years I vacationed elsewhere, but found no satisfactory replacement.

The fifth year after I found the cup I decided to stay home. There was no benefit in the idea other than curtailing my disappointment in another destination. I had a mortgage on a condominium in a suburb long past its 'trendy' days, and though I had an impressive collection of silent film memorabilia (most of it in storage), I had no creative hobbies—so there were no projects for me to 'finally have time for', either having to do with my property or any languishing avocation. I had no particular notion how I would occupy my time, and might have elected not to take my vacation at all if I hadn't been instructed otherwise.

Not that I would miss work. I had been bored at my job for some time by then—possibly from my first day. Oddly, the one aspect of weekdays I did not mind was my commute. The train ride between a place that was barely home and a job I didn't care for took about fifty minutes each way. You might expect such long, frequent forays into this transit limbo would exacerbate my general malaise, but I was never anxious on the rails. My line was crowded only close to the city, and that fraction went quickly. I read sometimes, or I noted the incremental change in the scenery through the seasons, or I smiled an umpteenth time at the strange stylistic transitions between songs listened to on a playlist arranged alphabetically by title.

As the train neared my stop to 'officially' commence my vacation from the rigmarole, I reached underneath my seat to retrieve my satchel. When I pulled it out, I felt some loose object drag along beside it, and I heard a dull plink of metal against the wall of the car. I thought something might have spilled from my bag, though I couldn't imagine what it might be. I bent forward and reached beneath my seat, but my hand found nothing. As the car was nearly empty and no one seemed to be watching, I slid to my knees and leaned my head to the floor.

Though the tell-tale inscription was pointed away from me, I had no doubt it would be there. I had inspected the cup for only a few minutes on a beach hundreds of miles away five years before, but the contours of the thing, even beneath the now-absent grit, were as familiar to me as the day I'd thrown it to the sand. There was a sudden sharpness to the moment, an acute dread and a falling away simultaneous with an odd exultation and a release of gravity, a sensory experience equivalent to the old 'rack-focus' camera trick common to suspense movies.

Surprising myself, I snatched it up immediately as though there was the danger someone else might do so before me. I was roused from my shock at its presence by the realization that the train had stopped. I barely made it out before the doors closed.

My mind raced, trying to define the implications of this thing in my hands finding me again so many years later. No, of course, I found *it*, I corrected myself. It was no use staring at the thing in the station. I needed private reflection to make sense of it. I looked around as though someone might be watching—who, or why, I had no idea. I squeezed the tiny thing between my forearms and my stomach like a running back with a football and kept it there the entire walk to my condo.

When I had the cup 'safely' home, I inspected it. It was, as I mentioned, clean of its former residue. What I had mistaken for tin was revealed as silver—'Sterling' was stamped on the bottom with the maker's mark 'WEB'. Gold wash inside the cup gleamed attractively. A quick internet search identified the manufacturer as the Web Silver Company of Philadelphia, in operation from 1950. The silver 'baby cup' was a novelty common to the era; Web Silver Co. sold especially at Wannamaker's department store. In its less-than-perfect state, I would be lucky to get thirty-five dollars for it. (Admittedly a small sum, but I confess to a moment's pleasure thinking on the beach-comber's oversight.) A search on the incomplete name was predictably futile.

The additional information was intriguing, but unhelpful. The cup belonged to the past. There was no cloudiness to my own past, so I didn't see how the object could illuminate any part of it. In the present, it might invoke someone else's nostalgia, but I had no stake in it. I likewise failed to see how someone else's dis-carded novelty could have any bearing on my future. And yet, here it was—too, too improbably for me to be contented with marveling at the coincidence.

I set it on a coffee table. I sat on the edge of the sofa and re-garded it. There were several unread magazines laid out next to it; these I pushed to the floor. Looking at it was like watching, when watching is waiting—as though I expected it to move or to speak, to indicate of its own accord what it wanted from me or to instruct me what I should do. It did not, of course. It merely rested there, not quite flat on the lacquered wood. It slowly dawned on me that I should not expect information to be forthcoming from the cup—whatever clues it conveyed were present and contained entirely in its small frame and the markings thereon. I resisted picking it up and turning it over again, as I couldn't imagine there was anything I could have missed before and there seemed to be no changes beyond a good cleaning made to the object in the five years since my last encounter. I reached for it several times with one or both hands, but I stopped before I touched it. Unwilling to disturb the cup, I turned myself over instead—I squirmed like a schoolboy at his desk, then bounced and wriggled from position to position over the sofa until I was dizzy. Until, again, as I had been at the beach, I was angry at the thing.

But what should I do with it? Why care at all, when it was so easily disposed of? This, I tried next, though the cup spent less time in the trash can then it did sitting on the coffee table. No, I could not brush aside the incredible coincidence of finding an object—*this* object, of which there could not be two. Indeed, the idea of aimless fortune was too incredible to entertain. It was clear other forces were at work, poking and provoking my course, but keeping silent their designs. I knew I must elevate the cup beyond its poor appearance, but I could not interpret the oracle.

I decided it was a seed. The bloom would be revealed, but for the time being, I should embrace my disquiet as a kind of initiation. I should display the object somewhere in my house and wait for subsequent understanding of its place in my life. Easily done. I put the cup on the mantle beneath the deco print, chiding myself for becoming overwrought.

I next moved it sometime after 3 a.m. that morning. Then once more before sun-up. And several times before noon.

I brushed my hands over my face and my arms repeatedly throughout the day, as though I'd walked into a cobweb I could not dislodge. When I felt particularly frustrated, I barked mono-syllabic nonsense to break the silence. My anxiety about the location of the cup seemed to lend credence to my conviction that its perfect placement was the condition that, once satisfied, would allow whatever next step that waited to finally occur.

I spent the entire two weeks of my vacation trying to find the right place for the cup. I felt ill by the third day and my degen-eration continued without relief. I was exhausted but could not sleep. I ate dry foods absentmindedly. I was distracted to the point I could not derive entertainment from any show I watched on TV, and every detail was lost to me the second a program concluded. I went out often, but never for long. A good feeling would come upon me in the open air, a feeling of clarity—into which erupted an inspiration of where the cup should go that seemed to perfectly resolve the matter. Eager to complete the puzzle and finally be free, I would immediately return home to affect the change. Needless to say, the inspiration never evoked the anticipated response.

Looks of concern and derision greeted me upon my return to work. Fortunately, routine bolstered my strength, if ever so slightly. I thought for the first time in two weeks of ridding myself of the thing, fate or fortune be damned. Whatever it asked of me was too much for me to give, and I began to plot my release of its influence. The idea of where to put the cup transitioned from placement in my home to disposal far away from it. I considered returning it to where I had found it, leaving it under the seat of the train. But I knew this would only lead to com-pulsive investigation beneath the seats (to see if I had escaped it), and though I might have little regard for the opinions of others, the compulsion would mean the destruction of my only respite—my commute.

Understand, I could not destroy it. I don't feel this was coward-ice. It was hard to trace the reason for this, but I could not reconcile myself with the idea that the thing needed destroying. Perhaps I felt it *could* yet mean something for me, even if I wanted nothing to do with it. Or perhaps it struck me super-stitiously—as though damaging the cup might do me even more harm than obsessing over it. It was better to be done with it peaceably. But where should I leave it?

I decided I must not think about it. If I could find no place for it in my home, then considering where to discard it in the wide world was sure to cripple me. Instead, I 'tricked' it. I set it once more on the mantle. And then I moved to the west coast.

I FOUND IT difficult to establish a new life in a new city. I could not get a good recommendation from my previous employer. I took on a string of menial jobs. The work was no better or worse than my lost profession, it simply paid less.

I lived in a walk-up apartment over a head shop. Both sides of the street were similarly occupied the length of the block: ground floor retail, two stories of habitation above. Catty-cornered pizzerias bookended my small world.

After three years, I was fortunate enough to secure a position processing customs forms for a shipping company. I worked in a cramped office in a warehouse, surrounded by three-part carbonless forms, but somehow returned to my apartment every evening smelling of fuel and fish.

One night, slightly later than usual, I walked down the block past one pizza place, past the travel agency, past the tattoo parlor. When I drew near the recessed door that would lead me to my modest abode, I chanced to glance in the window of the antique shop.

I know I must have cried out, though I'm sure I formed no intelligible word.

There it was, in the display, situated among the worthier and more attractive pieces and the hard-to-find nostalgic curiosities:

The cup.

I trembled from head to toe. Cold sweat seeped from my brow. I did not ask myself how it could be there, because *of course* it would be there—for up through the terror of what the thing might do to me came the feeling that *here* was the thing that had been missing from my life. Here was my second, my third chance! Here was my mystery again, waiting to reveal itself. If only I—if only I—if… *That* was the fear I had sought to define: that no matter what I did, I would fail, I would not discover the thing I needed to do to find the meaning of the thing in my life.

Because it must *mean* something.

It was marked at a low price. I could have gone in and bought it right away with what little I had in my pocket. It didn't matter if the shopkeeper didn't like the look of me and seemed to vacillate between coming out to shoo me away and calling the authorities to task them with it. My money was as good as anybody's. It was easily accomplished. But what then?

I relieved the shopkeeper of his decision and went to my squalor. I sat and tried not to consider every course and outcome in my head, to no avail. I went back into the street late that night and stared at the thing, barely visible in the darkened display. I looked at it and felt the weight of the thin metal in my memory. And I knew I must put opposite on the scale my endurance, and the weight I must measure was itself the act of measuring: how long could I go this time, before I decided I could not decide?

I think it is not necessary to describe how my body and soul withered near to nothing. It is likely understood already that I had several run-ins with the shopkeeper, the authorities, and a few innocent passers-by. My ranting was such that the shopkeeper never quite understood what object excited me so—or he knew, and refused to be bullied by my conduct into changing his display.

I tried to find apathy, convinced that that must be the answer, but I was not born with the temperament. It was a ruse, anyway, destined to fail—hoping that I could get what I wanted by fooling myself into not caring if I didn't. When that didn't work, I moaned and wailed every night in my rooms until I was evicted.

The following night, when I was sure the street was deserted, I kissed the glass. Only after did I understand it was a goodbye kiss.

Goodbye. I give up.

I do not know why I expressed the sentiment with affection. Perhaps it was an apology I made to myself.

I live on the ocean now. I go ashore only when ordered.

The next time I see the cup will be the last. My prayers now all beseech that the cup be kept from me for as long as possible.

And when my prayers are finished I think at length about what I might do between now and then.

Learning Not to Smile

Ralph Robert Moore

———— ◆ ————

BOTH HANDS ON the steering wheel, all four doors locked, windows rolled up. Block by block, more stores boarded, dogs wandering loose on the sidewalks, graffiti that made no sense, groups of men clustered at the street corners, watching you drive by. Not a place to run out of gas.

Claire was on her way deep down into the southern end of the city, to Father Panek Village.

Named after Monsignor Francis Panek, who had somehow gotten the funding together for the city's working poor. At one point, at the ribbon-cutting inauguration back in the nineteen-twenties, it probably did look like a village. Short blocks, small bungalows, front porches, people rocking, maybe a few teeth missing. Now it was row after row of three-story concrete project buildings for people who had no jobs, and had probably never held a job in their lives. Weeds growing out of the sidewalks, chain link fences pulled down.

She parked as close to Building B-6 as she could, to minimize the amount of time she'd be out in the open. Small canister of pepper spray in her purse.

Building B-6 was one of the older projects. A grass lawn past the parking lot, probably never walked on by anyone other than the mowing companies the city outsourced. On the sidewalk in front of the anonymous building, middle-aged Latino with a black moustache sitting behind a fold-down card table, selling corn on the cob from a large aluminum pot. But no customers. Steam.

He raised his right hand to his forehead, as if tipping a hat to her. "Senorita."

Her tight smile.

The sounds of loud TV programs as she hurried along the concrete sidewalk, past the curtained windows of the apartments. Large flower patterns. B-6-15. Knocked with her left hand.

Kept her right hand inside her shoulder-slung purse.

Eventually, the front door creaked open. Old woman behind the brass chain lock, looking out.

"Mrs. Sweeney? I'm Claire. The social worker assigned to your case."

The old woman closed the door in her face. Sound of the chain lock sliding off its groove. Front door opening. "Come in."

The apartment was actually quite large, considering it was for one person.

Wide living room with a TV, kitchen in back, bedroom on the left, and beyond that, at the rear of a short corridor with sliding doors for storage, a bathroom.

The two women, one old, one young, chose chairs in the living room. Sat down.

Claire noticed it right away. You couldn't help but notice. How to bring it up?

"Mrs. Sweeney?"

"Call me Hannah."

"Thank you. Hannah, I couldn't help noticing, if you don't mind me saying, that your stomach is quite protuberant."

Hannah's milky eyes, half here, in the living room, half somewhere else.

Her frail voice. "What does that mean?"

"You have a noticeable bulge in your stomach."

The old woman looked down at her seated body. At the prominent bulge in her abdomen. Milky eyes, filled with joy. "I'm pregnant."

Claire made a note. "Really. Well, congratulations. Looking at your file, I see you're ninety years old. Is that correct?"

Croaking voice. Smile. Yellow teeth. "It is."

"Isn't that kind of old to be pregnant?"

She smacked her lips, absent-minded. "I don't know. Is it?"

"May I ask who impregnated you?"

"Well, I don't know."

She tried a teasing approach. "Do you mean, you had so many sexual partners you're not sure which one is responsible for your pregnancy?"

Hannah sitting up, alert. "Oh, no! It just happened, dear. I woke up one morning, and I was with child."

Claire made more notes, pad wobbling on her upper crossed leg. "Have you had your abdomen x-rayed? Or undergone a sonogram? Just to see if there is, in fact, a fetus inside you?"

Hannah, vague. Wave of the wrinkled hand. "Why would I go to all that trouble? I can't afford doctors."

"What if the state were willing to pay for a doctor's appointment? So we could see inside your stomach and find out if you're truly pregnant, or if it's something else?"

"Well, what else could it possibly be?"

"Have you ever considered the possibility it may be a tumor growing in your stomach? That has distended your stomach, to where it might appear you're pregnant?"

"Oh, I am pregnant. I can feel the baby inside me."

"Would you be willing to have a doctor take an x-ray of your abdomen, just to be sure?"

"I don't know. That sounds kind of fancy."

"But would you agree it's rare for a ninety year old woman to be pregnant?"

"I don't know."

"What if a doctor were to examine you, and take an x-ray, or maybe a sonogram, and the state paid for all the cost? Wouldn't you want to know, definitively, that you are pregnant?"

Her old face. Black eyes, sagging mouth. "Well, I suppose so."

"Could I schedule a doctor's appointment for you, to take a look at your abdomen?"

"Would the x-ray harm my baby?"

"Absolutely not. It would just be a way of seeing what's truly inside you, then we can decide what's the best course of treatment, depending on what the x-ray shows us."

THERE WASN'T MUCH Claire liked about her job.

In college she didn't know what she wanted to do, just a fair-haired girl who liked to read and didn't hate her parents, so she majored in Education, with a minor in Psychology. Figured maybe she'd be a teacher. A girlfriend who was far more involved in campus activities, she was always on her hands and knees on the cheap carpet of her dorm room, writing big Magic Marker words on protest posters, had Claire sit in on some of her Political Science courses, then convinced her to sign up for some social engineering classes. It looked like a way to help people. "You never feel better than when you're helping others." That was the girlfriend's slogan. It appealed to Claire, because it was true.

After graduation, Claire was thrilled she got a job in a city-funded social intervention program. The offices were in a bad part of town, they never had enough supplies, not even coffee unless someone brought in a can for the office to share, but she'd be with young people determined to make a difference.

Except most of the middle staff in the office, the ones who really ran things, only a few years older than Claire, really didn't seem that interested in leaving this world a better place than they found it. What they really seemed interested in was running for Congress one day, like waiters think they're going to become actors one day. Although there were feminists in the office, males ruled. Sexism was rampant. "Tell me you drink pineapple juice every day and I'll go down on you." When she reported it to her superiors, her complaints were dismissed as her being "overly sensitive" and/or "misinterpreting the intent." There are bigger issues. Children are going to sleep hungry. Racism was also rampant, but on a much more subtle level. In the communal break room, no one eating any food item that had been touched by a black person's hands. An enforced hive mentality on social and political positions. Anyone who believes in God is pathetic. Everyone with an accent is a moron.

So she always looked forward, like a lot of the women did, to being out of the office, on calls. On her own.

But the calls were bruising. Didn't take long for her to realize she wasn't really helping that many people. Sure, she helped some, but in most cases she was just filling out forms about the damage that had already been done, and would be done again. Much like the cops she came to meet so often on these cases, who weren't preventing crime, just cleaning up afterwards.

And you sure learned a lot about what we were capable of, on these calls. Babies held down against a stove's burner because they wouldn't stop crying, old women pulled out of their wheelchairs and raped behind a bush, girlfriends' eyes that were gouged out because they may have been looking at another male in a fast food parking lot. Children who died of injected junk in a school restroom stall. All so awful it was almost comical in its absolute excess. Except it wasn't comical. Even the cops didn't make jokes.

THE NEXT WEEK, Claire came by again to pick up Hannah for her appointment. She should have arrived earlier. It took the woman half an hour to leave her apartment, between checking her hair in the mirror, trying to remember where she left her purse, going back for a third time to confirm the burners on the stove were off, raising her hand in the air as they were almost out the door to indicate she had to use her bathroom before they left.

Claire waited outside the closed bathroom door, decided to go back out into the living room, to give Hannah some privacy.

The TV was the only thing on the walls. No photographs, no cheap mass market paintings, no shelves with knick-knacks. Ear cocked for the sound of the knob turning, she went into the kitchen. Opened the small refrigerator's door. Bottle of ketchup, loaf of bread, iceberg lettuce that was browning, vials of insulin. In the freezer section above, vapor rolling out and two empty ice trays. In the cabinets, seven cans of soup, salt shaker, small jar of dried oregano. She wondered what the circumstances were that caused Hannah to buy this one herb.

Is this my future?

At the government clinic, Claire shielded the old lady from everyone milling around impatiently, got her a safe seat in one corner, near an end table with magazines spread out. "You sit right here, Hannah. I'm going to let them know you've arrived."

"Okay, dear."

Claire went down the rows of chairs and couches to the back of the reception area. No one in front of her in line just had a simple question for the one receptionist. All of them wanted to argue with the middle-aged woman about something. Several times she heard the woman say, "I'm not a doctor. I can't tell you anything about your symptoms. You'll have to wait for your appointment."

When it was her turn, Claire identified herself as a social worker. Gave her Hannah's name and appointment time.

"You're late."

"Ms. Sweeney took longer than I expected to get ready. I'm sorry."

The receptionist made an entry. "Okay, she's on the list."

"May I ask how long—"

"We're running late. There's about a two-hour delay." Looked behind Claire at the next person in line.

"The reason I ask is she's ninety years old, this is the first time she's been out of her apartment in a while, and she has what appears to be a particularly large tumor growing in her abdomen—"

"I'm not a doctor. I can't diagnose her condition."

"No, of course not. I like your bracelet! I don't think I've seen one like that before."

The middle-aged woman shot her a bored look. "Really, hon?"

Claire slunk back to the far corner.

"Do I get up now?"

"It'll be a little while. Would you like to read one of these magazines while we wait?"

"Can't read."

"Oh!"

"Do you have a man, dear?"

"No. No, I don't."

Hannah nodded to herself, lips downturned.

"Of course, these days, Hannah, women don't need a man."

"Okay." Hannah looked off into space.

THEY WERE FINALLY brought into the back examination cubicles about eleven in the morning. The black nurse, in her white uniform, was actually cheerful, a big plus. She spoke in a louder than normal voice. "Okay, Ms. Sweeney. I'm going to ask you to undress down to your underwear please, and put this hospital gown on you with the ties in front. Do you understand what you need to do?" The nurse looked at Claire.

"I'll help her."

"I'm going to come back for you in a short while, then we're going to take you and your friend to the x-ray area. Okay, Ms. Sweeney?"

"I suppose so."

"You have any boyfriends, Ms. Sweeney?"

"Don't be ridiculous."

"I don't know, I think you probably have a couple of beaus out there."

"Long time ago. When I was young." But it did seem to improve her mood.

At the x-ray area, they sat in the narrow corridor in two of a series of metal chairs, backs set against the corridor's walls. Most of the chairs were taken. Young girl with her mother, man in his twenties, sneakers spread on the floor in front of him, nursing his left wrist, old man attached to a rolling IV contraption, head of a needle stuck into his forearm.

The x-ray room itself was small, a bit larger than a closet. The technician asked Hannah to undo the ties at the front of her hospital gown. Place her abdomen against the x-ray machine. "Hold still! Don't breathe." Then place the left profile of her abdomen against the front of the machine; the right profile. "You wait back out in reception. We call you back later."

The reception area was half empty. Of course, it was the lunch hour.

Around two in the afternoon Hannah's name was called. She and Claire were escorted to a small examination cubicle, curtains drawn around the cubicle.

An hour later, the doctor showed up. Young, hurried. Ignored Hannah, who had fallen asleep on the examination table. Spoke to Claire. "Are you family?"

"I'm her social worker."

"So I can't have a discussion with you in the room."

"She's signed the necessary HIPAA forms."

The doctor slapped three x-rays up on the illuminated screen on one side of the cubicle. Looked up at them, stroking his chin. "Okay, let's see. Hah! How old is she?"

"Ninety."

"Really! Well, she does definitely have something inside her that seems to resemble a fetus. A late-term fetus, as a matter of fact."

Claire looked at the dark black and gray slides. Definitely, it was a baby-shaped form up inside Hannah's abdomen.

The young doctor looked annoyed. "How sure are you she's ninety?"

Claire, glancing down at the frail little woman asleep on the table, mouth open, wanted to answer, Doesn't she look ninety? But held her tongue. "She's ninety. Yup."

"Okay. Well, we need to do a sonogram."

"Can we do it today? While she's here?"

The doctor ran his eyes up and down Claire's crossed legs. "For you? I'll allow it." Big-toothed, ingratiating grin.

Back to the waiting area. Sitting side by side. The area was packed again, all the seats taken.

Hannah tugged Claire's sleeve. Brought her mouth to Claire's ear. Frightened whisper. "I want to go home and watch my TV."

"We will, Hannah. In just a little while."

The next time they were called back to the examination area, their new doctor was a little nicer. Indian or Pakistani.

Hannah lay on her back on the examination table. The doctor greased up her exposed abdomen. Hannah's head lifting in surprise off the examination table. Ran the rounded front of the sonogram probe over and around her upraised abdomen, like the planchette of a Ouija board. Looking up at a monitor mounted under the low ceiling. The gray and black third of a circle of the sonogram's signals. "Yes, there it is."

To Claire, it looked like a fetus.

"Well, the bad news is rather depressing?" He glanced across the small room at Claire. Kept his voice low. "It would appear the fetus is not moving. See? There is no heartbeat here. Where you would expect it. It is a miracle she has been pregnant, yes? But this fetus is not alive." Watching the monitor again as his right hand slid over the grease. "No, definitely not." Pulling the surgical gloves off his hands. "She will need a procedure."

THE PROCEDURE WAS scheduled for that Friday. Claire arrived at Hannah's apartment extra early, to give her time to be ready to leave. On the drive over to the hospital, Hannah put her wrinkled hand up on her side of the dashboard. "I want to take my baby home with me."

"I don't know if the hospital allows that, Hannah. It may be against the law."

Voice raising, angry, hopeless. "I don't care! It's my baby, and I want to take it home with me." She looked defiantly at Claire, jaw set, but of course, at that age, a set jaw means very little. Especially to people who work in a hospital.

"I'll do my best to get them to agree."

"It better Goddamn be your best."

Claire wasn't allowed to be present during the actual procedure, but she was permitted to participate in the brief pre-op consultation. The meeting took place in the doctor's office. The doctor, sitting behind his cluttered desk, pictures of sailboats on his walls, had the wide face of middle age, where from some angles the face still looks handsome. "We're going to consider going in through the vagina, but if it looks like that approach might be time-consuming, we'll remove the tissue through a strategic entrance in the abdomen. Are you prepared to stay with her a few hours back in her home, while the general anesthesia wears off?"

"Yes. Ms. Sweeney expressed a very strong desire to keep the fetus once it's removed."

"To do what? Sell it?"

"No. She's emotionally attached to it. It's a part of her."

Annoyed look from the doctor. "We have a protocol for excised tissue. It's either disposed of through our established procedures, or if there's something unique about it, as there is in her case because of her age, it's routed for further research. She can take pride in the fact she's furthering the cause of science. But she can't take the tissue home with her. Absolutely not. That's barbaric."

Claire waited in the outer reception area to be called back once Hannah's operation was finished. Alone in her chair, alone in a sea of chairs, most empty, she cried. For Hannah, for herself.

Two hours later, a door on the right opened. "Hannah Sweeney! Whoever came with her!"

Claire rose from her seat.

She thought she was being escorted to a post-op recovery room, but in fact she was taken to the doctor's office where she and Hannah had sat earlier.

After a ten minute wait, the same doctor entered the office. Sat again behind his desk. "Who are you, again?"

"Hannah's social worker. Is she okay? Did she survive the

surgery?"

"What do you know about her?"

"Not much. I've only been assigned to her for a few weeks."

"Does she have any history of mental delusions?"

"Nothing in her file. Nothing in my interaction with her suggested she had that issue."

Dismissive wave of the hand from the doctor. "You're not trained to spot it. That's the problem, we have untrained personnel handling these cases. Has there been any suicide ideation?"

"No." Feeling small.

"Of course, you wouldn't know what to look for."

Sat up in her chair, summoning some courage. "What's your point?"

Daggers from the doctor. "Your patient wasn't pregnant."

Claire was confused. "It was a tumor that looked like a baby?"

"There's no tumor. She had a plastic doll inside her abdomen."

She lost her resentment. "What?"

"Yeah! She apparently forced a life-sized plastic doll of a baby up inside her, and God knows how she managed to distend her vagina that wide, to make her appear to be pregnant. Is she an alcoholic? Does she take any psychotropic drugs, prescription or illegal?"

Claire sat silent. Face cold.

"She really needs to be put under observation. But that's your job. This has been a complete waste for me. I was all set to publish a paper on a ninety year old being pregnant. Now she's just some senile woman who decided to shove a doll up her cunt. Sorry. Language. But I'm extremely disappointed."

"Does that mean she can take her baby home with her?"

"Excuse me?"

"Since it turns out there's no tissue involved, it's a plastic doll she bought with her own money, is she allowed to bring the doll home with her?"

"Are you fucking kidding me?"

"Your fee is being paid by Medicare. Do you want me, or my Director, to file a federal claim against you with Medicare?

Language?"

Hannah came out of the general anesthesia enough to where she could dress herself, with Claire's assistance.

"Where's my baby?" Black eyes darting around in a panic. "Where's my baby?"

"I have your baby over there, Hannah. In that chair. See? Once we have you dressed, I'll take you and your baby back to your home."

The hospital staff hadn't washed the blood off the doll that had been inside Hannah, but the old woman clutched its plastic curves to her breast anyway on the long drive back to her home. She looked happier than Claire had ever seen her.

Once back at the apartment, Hannah bustled around, making a space on her bed for where the baby would sleep, laying down a doubled-over bath towel, fetching a bag of plugs she had evidently bought recently to push into the rooms' wall sockets, to baby-proof her home. Claire offered to wash the blood off the doll, but Hannah, with the pride of a new mother, insisted on doing that herself, carrying her baby to the kitchen counter, laying it down carefully on its plastic back, cooing to it while she adjusted and readjusted the hot and cold taps on her kitchen sink until she had a lukewarm flow. She wiped the blood off the stiff limbs and head with paper towels, pink water swirling down the stainless steel sink's drain.

Once the baby was cleaned and dried, Hannah carried it against her bosom into the living room. Settled into her favorite chair, baby in her lap. Stroked its plastic head.

And looking down, started crooning to it in a high, frail voice.

"Down in the valley
There are apples in the river
Bobbing past the blue birds,
Floating past just you and me."

Claire was surprised by the utter sweetness on Hannah's face as she sang. The raised, almost bald eyebrows, the way she'd try so sincerely to reach the higher notes. She could see the face of the happy little girl Hannah had been, long, long ago, singing with her family.

Watching all this, the joy, the extreme care, Claire decided, You know what? I can have a talk with Hannah some other time. Let her be content for now.

Once Hannah was snuggled in bed with her baby, squeezing her eyes at Claire, Claire turned off the bedside lamp, said good-night to them both, and left, making sure she locked the front door behind her.

SHE WAITED A week before going back to Hannah's apartment. Not always, but sometimes, it helps to let someone come to reality on their own.

She didn't know what to expect when she knocked on the door. No answer? (She'd have to call the police, let their wide blue shoulders be the first to access the apartment, to locate where Hannah or her body was); Hannah answering weak and forlorn, the doll in the trash with empty soup cans? (She might have to recommend a mental/nervous evaluation, which could mean Hannah being placed in a hospital for observation, and losing her apartment.)

The front door swung inwards. Hannah in the doorway.

Claire looked quickly to see if anything was in the old woman's hands; tried to judge the woman's emotional state.

Hannah took a moment, then grinned. "There you are!"

The doll was propped up in one of the living room chairs, in front of the TV. Rich women with horrible plastic surgeries screaming at each other during a dinner service of what looked like salads.

Claire accepted a glass of water from her hostess. "So how are you?"

Hannah clasped her old hands together. "I am so happy!"

"How's your son doing?"

"Look at him!"

Claire took a seat. "Well, he certainly looks healthy. Are you breast feeding him?"

Hannah, thumb-pressing the volume button on her TV remote to turn down the weeping and name-calling, turned shy. "I don't give him breast milk." That long distance stare. Lowering of the wrinkled face. "My breasts have long dried out." So, some sense of reality. "I give him store-bought milk. Warmed on the stove."

"Can I watch you give him the milk?"

Closed-eye shake of the head. "He prefers to eat when it's just me and him."

"Okay. What's your baby's name?"

Sly smile. "That's the secret."

"It is? Why's it a secret, Hannah?"

Troubled look. "There are people around the world who are searching for him. They want to find him. Destroy him."

"Why would they want to do that, Hannah?"

Raised her frail chin. "There are more things in heaven and earth than are dreamt of in your philosophy. Are you enjoying your water?"

"He's probably old enough now that maybe a pediatrician should check him out. To make sure he's developing normally."

Eyes closing again, set mouth. Head swinging left, right. "He's fine."

"You're not a doctor though, Hannah."

"So when do I start getting benefits for my boy?"

"Benefits?"

"I had a son! If someone is on assistance, and they have a child, their allowance is automatically increased, to cover the costs of that child."

Did Hannah painfully shove a plastic doll up into her vagina, past her vagina up into her abdomen, because she thought it would increase her monthly stipend?

Which kind of disappointed Claire. She was sympathetic towards a Hannah who was crazy but sincere. She didn't know how she felt about a Hannah who was just conniving, trying to beat the system like so many others.

The evening ended on a flat note. After Hannah brought up the increase in benefits a few more times, Claire said she would look into it, although there was really nothing to look into, but worse than that, she felt like she was losing a friend. After she said goodbye to Hannah at the front door, watching the door shut, hearing the latch slide into place, she turned to walk to her car feeling depressed.

She was sprawled on the sidewalk, on her back. Looking up, dazed. Again, the tug at her right hand, until she finally released the grip on her purse. Footsteps running away. "Don't say nuthin!"

Her phone was in her pocket, thank God. Bloody finger punching 911.

Tried to get to her knees. Not successfully. Like her rising hips weighed five hundred pounds, rolling around like bowling balls.

The police took twenty minutes to get to the projects. A long time, when you're throwing up on a concrete sidewalk, and you have a dream remembrance there's something wrong with your face.

After the police arrived, black shoes all around her eyes, ordering her to stay on the sidewalk where she was, another twenty minute wait for the ambulance. By now, there were a lot of blood asterisks on the sidewalk's rough surface, from whatever had happened to her face (because all the red was directly below her raised head).

The confusion of having to explain to so many people, even a few women, that she didn't have her medical card because the card was in her purse, and her purse had been stolen. White walls of an underground hospital corridor around her, sliding past, as she was rolled on a gurney to a pale blue door getting bigger and bigger, all the way at the far front of the gurney, between her panty-hosed feet.

Someone who was male but who turned out not to be a doctor (she never found out exactly what his title was) told her, holding a clipboard in his hands in her recovery room, that she had some trauma to her face resulting from her attack, and that as a result of that assault her nose was broken, and she had lost three of her front teeth. After she kept insisting, he reluctantly found a mirror and handed it to her.

Her face, but her nose in a white-bandaged beak. Her forced smile, but a big gap in the row of teeth. Plus it looked like gum damage where the teeth were knocked out, thick black threads of sutures sewn deep into the pink, criss-crossing each other in triangles.

"Should have just given him your purse."

She was discharged the following day. For her severe facial pain, the woman who rolled her to the elevators in a wheelchair suggested she take over-the-counter aspirin. A woman she worked with at the social services office, who had once offered Claire half her sandwich in the breakroom, which made Claire think she might be one of the few people in the world who would be willing to help her, who she called from her hospital bed, was waiting outside. Eyes looking a little put out.

Of course, when Claire arrived back at her apartment, the place had been robbed. Because she had her keys in the purse. Two jagged holes in the white wall where her TV had been attached. Refrigerator door hanging open, most of the food missing. (And she remembered: She was going to cook a rib eye steak when she got home that night from Hannah's.) Her bedroom closet empty, hangers still on the rod or lying in a geometric mess on the closet's floor. Laptop nowhere to be found. Someone had ejaculated on her pillow.

She took some vacation days, sitting in a chair in her living room. One book or another in her lap, because her TV and laptop were gone, but not reading. At some point each day eating another slice of the pizza she ordered delivered her second day home, having to cut up the triangle into small squares she'd chew with her back molars, crying.

It was hard.

She went back to work the following Tuesday. Had to get out of the apartment. A couple of people at work asked how she was. Everyone had trouble understanding her. Because of the injury to her mouth. To where they'd get a bit annoyed.

More than anything else, more than fear, or anger, or self-pity, what she felt most was shame. Shame that she had been victimized. Shame that she had to keep her lips together, so she didn't show the big humiliating gap in her teeth (and more than anything else in America, missing teeth means poverty.) Quite a few people wanted to see, though. And were annoyed when she didn't open her mouth for them.

During lunch on Thursday she went to a dentist for a consultation. Sat in the padded chair, jiggling her right hand on the arm rest. X-rays were taken. She realized she'd be late going back to the office. The dentist seemed like a nice guy. Professional. His assistant was sympathetic. Putting her hand on Claire's upper arm as Claire told her story.

"Okay, so we have some good news. Despite the trauma, your maxilla was not broken. We can do three implants. It would be an endosteal implant for each tooth, which is the best kind of implant, drilling a titanium screw into each site up into the bone, then stitching everything shut and waiting for osseointegration to take place, which is usually a few months. Then we reopen your gums with a scalpel and attach the actual teeth replacements. They'll function like normal teeth once everything heals."

Claire in the padded chair, circular light above her shining down on her mouth, the meekest she's ever been in her life. "How much would that cost?"

"I can do all the surgeries, the screw placements, and the crowns for twelve thousand."

She wanted to cry. "I can't possibly afford that."

He nodded. "That's okay. It's the best solution, but we realize that's kind of expensive for a lot of budgets. As an alternative, I can do a fixed bridge. The thing is—" He pointed his right pinky inside her mouth—"We really don't want to use this incisor here on the left side of the trauma as an anchor, because incisors can't really bear the repeated stress of a fixed three-tooth bridge. We'd want to extract that incisor, then anchor a four-tooth fixed bridge to your two canines. They'd provide much better support, long-term. You'd have two anchors, and four pontics. Cost-wise, we're talking about five thousand dollars."

"Is there anything else I can do?"

"Well, you could go with a removable bridge. It's essentially a partial denture. You have to take it off to clean it. A lot of people take it out before they eat. It's basically cosmetic. That'd run you, in your case, about fifteen hundred dollars to two thousand dollars."

She'd think about it. The consultation cost her two hundred and fifty dollars.

YEARS WENT BY. She learned not to smile. Hard at first, then after a while, you know what? Not so hard.

Quit her job at the agency. Took too much from her to pull into a parking lot in a bad part of town, and they were all bad parts of town, and then be expected to get out of the metal protection of her car and walk, exposed, across grass to her case file's front door. Instead, she started an online consulting business where she helped people prepare applications for social assistance. Most of her clients were lawyers, farming out their different tasks. It was a living. Pretty good living.

She joined several online dating services. Always looking for big men who clearly just wanted sex. She could tell by the arrogance of the faces on their profiles if they were the type of man she was seeking. Someone who'd treat her like something long and soft with three holes, and liked to be a little rough, fingers clamped on the back of her head, meaty hand spanking her ass while he fucked her. She enjoyed the humiliation, appreciated the sated laziness of them not getting off the sofa after she dressed and turned back in their direction, hand on the doorknob. Them searching the cushions of the couch for their TV remote. Those were the best. Relaxed her.

About six years after her assault, she was driving around aimlessly one day, as she often did, listening to the radio, mostly rap, when she realized she was back in the neighborhood where Hannah lived.

She couldn't possibly still be alive, could she?

Broad daylight, but she left her purse in the car, carried the pepper spray openly in her right hand.

Knocked on the front door.

Already phrasing in her mind the explanation she'd give to whomever the new tenant was.

An old woman swung the door inwards.

Milky eyes looking down at Claire's hands. "Where's my food?"

"Hannah? Do you remember me?"

Hannah taking a step back. "Oh, dear. I thought you were the delivery girl."

"Do you remember me? Claire?" Hesitated. "I was with you when you had your baby." She realized it was important to her that Hannah remembered her.

Long stare up at Claire's face. "You were the one who didn't have a man!"

That's what she remembers of everything they went through together? "May I come in?"

"Sure, yeah." Shuffling to one side, to let her pass through the doorway.

The living room was dark. TV on the wall looking extra bright.

Claire glanced around, looking for the doll. Didn't see it. "What happened to your baby?"

Hannah trudging back to her easy chair. "He's in his room, resting. He was up late last night."

Claire put the pepper spray into her skirt's pocket. "Can I pop my head in, just to say hello?"

"Yeah, guess so. Don't wake him."

She went down the short hall to the doorway on the left.

On the bed, a body on its back. She tip-toed in a few steps, to see better.

A larger doll than before. Doll of a six year old boy. In pajamas.

Plastic head on the pillow. Fixed eyes staring forward.

Jumped when she realized Hannah was directly behind her. The woman knew how to be silent. "He was up late last night, writing. He's resting now."

"What does he write about?"

She clacked her dentures in her mouth. "Redemption. Pages and pages. The paper gets expensive! But I don't care. I love him."

They went back to the living room. "You want some water, dear?"

"Okay. Should I get it?"

"I will."

Slow trudge towards the kitchen.

Claire raised her voice, to be heard. "Is he in school yet?"

But no reply.

On the wall TV, images of bombs falling. Big, big plumes of smoke rising from buildings.

"Here you go, dear."

Claire set the water on a side table. "Is your son in school yet?"

Firm shake of the head. "He teaches."

"Really. To whom?"

"The neighborhood kids. For now."

"How interesting. Did you ever get the extra benefits from government assistance for your son?"

Bitterness. "They're tight with their little pennies."

"Guess they have to be careful. It is taxpayer's money. Did you know I was assaulted the last night I saw you?"

"Always wondered why you never showed up again."

"Yeah. See what they did to my teeth?" Her first smile in a long time.

"Was you raped?"

"What? No, thank God."

"There's a lot of assaults around here. My son will change that."

"Really, Hannah? A plastic doll is going to make things right in the neighborhood?"

"My crowning achievement. To have birthed him. He came out so calm. Didn't even cry."

Claire was surprised at the amount of anger she felt towards the older woman. Picked up her water glass, the equivalent of counting to ten. Took a sip.

Spat it back into the glass. "What is this?"

"It's water, dear."

"No, it's not." Cautiously sniffed the contents of the glass. Took a wary taste. "It's wine."

"I gave you water."

Should she? Shouldn't she? Looked across the dim living room at where Hannah sat. "You know on some level you're crazy, right?"

Hannah put her wrinkled hands on the arms of her easy chair. "Think you better leave."

So it was like that. The rest of her life had to be better, right? Jesus, she remembered the daydreams she had as a little girl, looking up at the clouds.

Hannah opened her front door. Overhead, a smoggy sky. As always. In the distance, police sirens. As always. From a block away, a scream. As always. Claire retrieved her pepper spray from her pocket. It was getting dark again.

This could have been a much nicer world, in a lot of ways.

Hannah poked Claire in her back.

She turned around.

The old woman's milky eyes, filled with glee. "He is risen."

FISHER AND LURE

Christopher Burke

———— ✦ ————

SHELLS AND SHALE crackled beneath my shoes as I continued my ceaseless walk. The view in front of me was littered with detritus and dead things. But it appeared that I was not the only living being on that lonely beach.

I couldn't make out any details, but a short figure had emerged from nowhere and seemed to be approaching. My instinct was to turn to the left and move off of the rocky beach. I'd become so un-accustomed to the company of others that I was no longer certain I wanted it, now that it was advancing toward me.

I stopped, looked around at a landscape I'd already been looking at for hours. The simple choice of whether to continue or diverge from my endless path was enough to paralyze me for a moment.

The child grew steadily closer, moving with an eerie speed that seemed unnatural. I could see now that it was a boy, about seven years old, with wispy blond hair. It seemed he had made my decision for me; I started to walk away from the water, hoping to get off the beach before he got too close.

That's all I need to deal with now, some obnoxious kid who got lost, I thought. I couldn't take him to the police. I wouldn't know what the hell to do with him. And I've never been good with kids, anyhow.

Before I had finished my train of thought and gotten very far, the boy was suddenly at my side, tugging my arm.

"Mister, mister!" he shouted. He was dressed in strange clothing that I couldn't recognize or even begin to describe. He waved a beaten-up old shoe in one of his hands. How did he move so fast? He was hundreds of feet away a few seconds ago.

"What? What is it, kid?" I asked.

"Is this your shoe? I found it over there. On the ground, see?" He pointed back in the direction from which he'd come, as though I could tell where, in the miles of beach stretching before us, he might have picked it up.

"Nah, it ain't mine. I got both of 'em right here," I said, pointing down at my feet, both of which clearly had a shoe on. "Now run along. You shouldn't be going around talkin' to strangers."

"Oh, *pffft* on you," he said. "I talk to strangers all the time. Everybody's a stranger. 'Specially here. Say, who do you think it came from?"

"Kid, I have no idea. It's just an old wet shoe. The hell you want to pick up nasty old shoes for, anyway? Say, where's *your* shoes, kid?—Hey, you're bleeding!"

The boy looked down dismissively, as though the blood was either not real or didn't belong to him. As though he wasn't in any pain at all.

"Hey, Mister, why don't you come see where I found it."

He tugged at my arm.

"No, kid, I can't just now."

"Pleeeease?"

He pulled on my arm with a surprising strength. Startled, I stumbled forward.

"It's just a shoe," I said.

"I knoooow that, mister, but I wanna show you where I found it."

Christ, I thought with a sigh.

"All right, all right. Yer gonna yank my arm out. Cool it."

He continued to drag me forward, even though I was moving willingly enough. No matter what, though, he seemed to move too fast for me. I wanted to stop him out of concern for his bloody feet, but he didn't leave me much room for protesting and he didn't seem to care anyway. His feet got bloodier and bloodier as we breezed over the rocks and shells, but he never seemed to feel it.

"You ever met The Fisher?" the boy asked.

Fisher, not fisherman. Odd way of putting it.

"Kid, I've met plenty of fishermen in my time."

"No, no, The Fisher. He's usually down this way. Maybe it's his shoe!" he said, excited.

"Can't say I have," I answered. "So if it's his shoe, why don't you take it to him and leave me out of it?"

"Becaaaaause," the kid said. "I'm afraid of The Fisher. Won't you protect me?" His tone was some kind of saccharine caricature, like a young boy in a '50s sitcom.

"Afraid? Why?"

"Cus, I don't want him to catch me."

"Catch you, huh? Kid, the way you move, nobody could catch you if they tried," I retorted. "Look, I hope you get that shoe back to your Fisher, or whatever, but I really gotta get goin.'"

I yanked my arm violently free of his grip. Parts of my skin ripped off in his hand and stuck to the little nails. Jesus, this creep's strong. I stalked off, confused and a little hurt. I wandered aimlessly for a few seconds and before I knew it, the kid appeared, practically out of nowhere, right in front of me, dangling the shoe.

"Pleeease, just help me get the shoe back to The Fisher," he said. I ignored him and changed direction, and he would fall out of sight for a few moments, but then he popped back into my path, again seemingly out of nowhere.

"He's hungry, and he's real down on his luck. Hasn't caught anything all day," the boy said with an exaggerated pout.

What the hell is this kid's deal? I thought.

"All right, all right! Let's just get this over with. Then will ya leave me alone already?" I said.

He didn't respond, just latched onto me again with those nails and ridiculously strong grip. He dragged me again, almost powerfully enough that I couldn't have resisted if I'd wanted to without ripping out more skin and maybe even a chunk or two of flesh deeper down. We made a beeline again for some distant spot on the waterline, presumably wherever this Fisher character was lurking without his damned shoe.

"Hey, hold on a sec. You got something stuck to ya."

I reached out at something I had noticed, a whisper of light, flashing silver. Some kind of thin filament caught in his hair.

"Don't worry about that, Mister," he said, sustaining the rapid pace as I stumbled after him.

I continued to fret with the filament, but it led out in front of him and I couldn't reach well enough to get a grasp of the little bit of string or wire or whatever it was. We drew closer and closer to the water line, approaching what must have been the point at which the boy had first entered my vision.

"Hey, hey, hold up!" I yelled. He was leading us straight to the water, with no sign of this Fisher guy.

The boy ignored me and kept going, until I yanked my arm free. This time, I felt a good bit of pain as the boy's claw-like nails refused to budge even a little, and a hunk of flesh was torn out of my arm.

"You little shit!" I yelled. "The fuck's the matter with you?"

He didn't answer, only came back and waved the shoe at me.

"We're takin' this back to The Fisher!" he yelled. "He hasn't caught anything all day and he's gotta eat!" He waved the nasty, wet shoe around and stomped his feet, but his movements were all off, unnatural somehow. I noticed again the flicker of silver in his hair and squinted my eyes.

Fishing line? I wondered. Maybe a stray bit caught in his hair when he was hanging out with Fisher, before he started annoying me. The filament remained taut in the strong breeze, but I still couldn't quite get a grip on it. Besides, this kid was creeping me out and my arm was bleeding severely. I started walking away again.

"Quit flopping around, fishy!" he yelled. He appeared in front of me again, latched onto my arm, and I shouted in pain. "Don't you want to get this back to The Fisher?" he asked.

"There ain't nobody around here, you little creep," I said.

"The Fisher is," he said. "He's close."

"I'm tellin' ya—"

"The Fisher's here. He's close," the boy repeated. He dragged me again, and if my arm hadn't still been in a great deal of pain, I'd have resisted harder or yanked it away again. But I didn't want a repeat of the injury I'd just sustained, and I wasn't about to lower myself to the level of hitting some kid that I didn't even know. I knew myself to be a pretty rotten person, but even I wasn't quite prepared to do that.

"The Fisher's here. He's close," the boy said yet again as we started down toward the water. The silver filament stuck out before him again and I finally managed to grasp it. It didn't move though, and it remained taut on a path between the boy and some point in the water. He didn't seem to notice it, and we were soon moving too fast for me to think about it.

"Yeah, yeah, the damned Fisher is close. I get it."

His hooked fingers dug into my flesh and we once again resumed our rapid pace to the water's edge. I instinctively kicked off my own shoes as they started to get wet, but I was moving too fast to look back and make sure they landed on dry sand. He pulled and pulled until we were both in the water, and it was soon up to his waist. The boy appeared not to care, and I seemed to have lost the ability to resist. My entire arm was on fire, as he'd worked his claw-fingers deeper and deeper into my flesh. Christ, this kid's powerful, I thought.

"Hey, hey, hey!" I said. "This is far enough."

The water was up to the boy's waist and up to my knees, but he wasn't stopping or slowing down.

"This is ridiculous!"

"The Fisher's here. He's close."

The silver line coming out of the boy's head flickered in the light.

The other end of it disappeared into the water. He moved deeper and deeper into the waves, despite my resistance. It seemed the closer we got to our destination, the more powerful he became.

I was beyond panicked, but I couldn't stop our forward momentum as I was pulled forward with him, old nasty shoe in one hand and my arm in the other.

The kid's head disappeared under the water and he soon brought me with him. He turned back and yelled something at me. It was impossible to hear clearly under the water, but he was close enough that I thought I made out one word: "Here!"

I started flailing wildly, completely out of my element and terrified. My body didn't know how to operate under the water and I was beginning to run short of breath.

I started to see spots before my eyes and I knew that I was not going to be able to wrench myself free. A huge hand came into my spotty vision, gripping the silver filament that protruded from the boy. He yanked the silver line forward, and we both came with it, the boy now having gone limp like an inanimate, empty human-sack.

The last thing I saw before the spots overwhelmed my consciousness was a huge bucket underwater, into which I was deposited alongside the rest of what I assumed was The Fisher's catch so far for the day.

THE DEATH OF SOCRATES

Michael Wehunt

———— ◆ ————

CARA SAT ON the edge of the bed, listening to her husband murmur under the floor. Her hand moved to the lamp but left the room dark for a moment. She felt the vibration of his words through the old oak floorboards, through her bare feet, through the hum of the space heater glowing red against her legs.

Something in his voice rooted her there. It flowed almost like water through pipes, unbroken as a litany. His side of the bed had not been slept in, the covers smooth under the goose pillow. Cara scrubbed her hands up and down her face. She'd been dreaming of the Causeway they'd walked last fall in the hushed red and orange of upstate Vermont, and now she waited for all the months between to bleed back into the darkness of the room. It was only Ethan, she told herself. He was probably just confused again.

Twice last week he'd done this, but in those cases it had been before bed, moments after he would have heard the creak of the mattress as she settled onto it. Both times he'd mumbled a sentence or two and then climbed back down to the first floor. Tonight he hadn't come to bed at all.

She glanced at the glowing hands of the clock. Half past three. Her husband's voice went on in its stream.

"Ethan, stop it," she said, more harshly than she'd meant. "It's not funny."

Her feet found her slippers in the same instant her hand found the twist on the lamp. She stomped on the floor a single time but his murmur continued. A knot of guilt, even shame, hardened in her stomach. Ethan was *sick*, what was she thinking?

She swore under her breath, grabbed her robe off the closet door and went into the hallway. "Ethan," she called from the staircase, "come to bed, honey." The first floor was stifled with dark. Not even the familiar wedge of porch light angled through the panes high in the front door. A blanket of quiet. Whatever he was doing, she couldn't hear it from the stairs.

The palm of her sliding hand squeaked against the railing and startled her. The steps sighed under her feet. She passed through the gulf of the living room, the grace of muscle memory guiding her around the end table beside the sofa. Ahead of her loomed the dim shape of the office doorway, like black paper laid against black felt. The soft half-whisper of his voice was even fainter down here, and not as close as she'd hoped.

"Ethan," she said, and waited, hugging the robe shut. "Quit it, Ethan. Get out here. Now."

He kept on speaking, and she again thought of a litany, a looping prayer. She reached around the doorframe and fumbled for the switch. The light snapped on and the room was empty. Ethan's laptop was closed, his usual mess of papers and notebooks covering the desk around it. A stepladder lay overturned on the floor.

Cara looked up at the ceiling panel they'd only discovered in June, when they decided to have an office for Ethan here rather than a junk closet. It led to a short crawlspace between floors, a pocket that stretched from the center of the house to the eastern wall. The sliding panel was partly open, uncertain.

She stood below it a full five minutes, until she heard a drumming burst of thumps and choking wails. Then nothing. It was the tumor, she had to remember that. He could be having a seizure up there. She wanted to pick the ladder up, to shout his name, anything to help him. Instead she crept back upstairs. The quiet was much louder than the murmur had been. Not even her sobs could fill it. She turned on the TV's white noise and dry swallowed an Ambien.

SHE OPENED HER eyes to find Ethan in bed, snoring in his cartoon way, flutelike. He lay on his side, hands loose fists under his chin, face slack and peaceful as a toddler's. Light came strong through the sheer cream curtains and his old scar curled like a hook from his graying sideburn.

She stared at the ceiling and tried to find some comfort in its rough whorls of plaster. As if written there were the words he'd been saying in that dead, chanting voice. Or why he would crawl up between the floors in the first place.

At seven she got up to shower. He was still asleep when she left for work. She made it through another day with her fifth-graders while her Zen face slowly broke apart. It was hard not to congratulate herself for leaving the Ambien at home. She braved the traffic, got dinner started, turned the space heaters back on to save money.

Ethan was distant, airy. "It's better than yesterday," he said, but still he used his headache to bat her questions about last night aside. She watched him sneak his fingertips up against his temples, prodding the hollows there. A clock in every room measured out his time.

CARA SAT IN the dark again. She held the remote and the blank TV threw back the pale green arms of the alarm clock. Under the floor, Ethan's voice was a little louder tonight. A prayer, surely.

It had been twenty-four endless days since they'd learned his tumor was a level three. The sharp, pretty face of Dr. Furst calmly shoveling out grave words. Brain cancer. Chemo. Inoperable. Odds slim enough for Cara to make an appointment with her psychiatrist for her old friend Valium, but just hopeful enough to talk herself into canceling it from her car in front of his office.

She slid off the bed and knelt on the floor, as though intending her own prayer. With her ear pressed to the floorboards, she could nearly pick out a word or two. The top of her head grew unbearably hot from the heater and she climbed back to her feet.

She had to sit him down and talk. She needed to know what he thought he was doing up in the ceiling, under the floor. If he was hurting, and what she could do. She wanted to hear her voice say she was there for him, regardless of the fact that she already felt herself losing touch.

They'd just started trying to have a baby after the school year ended. The timing was right, the stars had finally aligned for them, until Ethan's headaches started. The unfairness of it was like her own tumor.

And below her feet, the rhythm of his voice. Something close to music.

"I FEEL GREAT, love. I even feel like I could work." The look on his face when he said it broke her heart, but she surprised herself by believing him. He was almost younger, somehow. More vital.

She turned away. It was Saturday morning and she stood at the stove frying eggs and bacon in the same skillet, the way he liked. He sipped his decaf and leafed through a magazine. For a few seconds she could imagine it was still June. A new start and a home they hadn't quite settled into yet. It had been a wonderful summer but it felt years gone now.

Her mouth opened and closed, the words she wanted to say clumping together inside. She laid the bacon out on paper towels to drain while she peppered the eggs. Then everything was on plates and she couldn't put off sitting with him anymore.

He ate with a vigor she hadn't seen in months, hardly pausing long enough to compliment the food before he stuffed more in. She watched him, traced the lines of him with her eyes. In the morning light his skin looked fresh, the hooking scar dim.

"Ethan," she said, snagging on his name and then pushing herself on. "I need to know what you're doing at night."

He swallowed and stared at his fork. A string of yolk slowly dripped to the plate. "Sorry if I worried you," he said. "I'm just doing some thinking."

"Out loud?"

"Well, meditating, then." He finally looked up at her. "It's nothing, some words to help clear my head."

"What words?"

"Stuff from one of my books. Socrates talking about what happens to the soul and body after—you know."

"Okay, most people would choose Jesus over Socrates, so that's good. But why do you need to creep me out under the floor to do it? It's not exactly normal and—" She stopped and bit her lip hard. She wasn't being fair.

"It calms me," he said, watching his plate again. "It might not sound like it when I'm in there, but it's fine. Just let me have this." His words reminded her of when the shoe had been on the other foot, sitting at this very table in another house discussing the pills he'd found in her underwear drawer.

She stared at him, feeling the angry tightness around her mouth but unable to stop it. "You promise you're feeling okay? The sounds you make scare me."

"Yes." He reached across and picked up her hand. "You'll see."

This was her cue to be the loving wife. The support system, the best friend. She managed to find a weak smile and a squeeze of his fingers before getting up and raking her plate off into the trash.

THE MORNINGS THAT followed softened her. A couple of them began with Ethan's hand pulling her out of sleep and on top of his warm body. Years melted away with him inside her. Other days she still had to rush to work after simply watching the smooth peace of his face as he slept.

But in the evenings his headaches returned, regular enough to set clocks by. A quarter to nine and he'd start rubbing his temples and the rich, chatty dinner they'd shared would turn sour in her stomach as she sat helpless against his pain.

And in the nights, somewhere in their smallest hours, she would wake to his voice beneath her. She started sleeping with the bedroom TV tuned to one of the audio-only music channels, but Ethan woke her up anyway. His voice grew louder as the nights stacked up past a week.

She took him to the hospital and graded book reports while Ethan was prodded and stuck into machines. Dr. Furst stood before the spectral CAT scan chart and told her they shouldn't get their hopes up, it was important to remain realistic. Cara nearly had to wrench from her that Ethan's tumor appeared to have shrunk dramatically.

"It's still there," the doctor said, placing a fingertip beneath a black smudge in the X-ray. "But it's over eighty percent smaller. I admit it's remarkable. We've run some more tests and I want to get his tumor markers again. So until we learn from those let's keep chemo on the board."

"He's been telling me how good he feels," she said, staring at the smudge. She could have believed it was a piece of dust on the camera lens, if not for the blackened golf ball shape that had been in the precise spot just last month.

"No headaches?" Dr. Furst had taken her glasses off and was pinching the bridge of her nose as if she had her own migraine.

"No, he still gets one every night, before…before bed. But from morning until dinner he's a different person. The Ethan I met, almost." She tried to bring up the crawlspace, the murmuring beneath her floor, but she couldn't bear to upset the flutter of hope lodged in her chest. Her eyes welled up instead.

"Just try to stay grounded, Mrs. Petrakos. I wish I could tell you more today, but we'll talk again after the weekend and figure this out."

Cara stepped back into the waiting room and kissed her husband, cradled his head in her hands as though she could truly love that speck out of his brain. The belief that it could get even smaller settled down into her stomach. It nestled against the renewed hope for a baby. It felt like light.

SHE HELD ONTO that light, tried to stay in every moment with Ethan. He gained a few of his pounds back. They went for bundled-up walks that grew shorter as the days did. They shopped for red meat and leafy greens. They watched too much TV until the inevitable headache came.

But too often she felt as if her favorite music were playing in another room, and her mind wandered from his conversation, or more frequently whatever was on Netflix, to pick out its melodies. Even if his tumor really was shrinking, it could just come back. She knew that. And so it was easier to bury herself in the rhythms of other times.

In the pall of the cancer and the early St. Louis winter, their trip to Vermont last October was never far from her mind. It was like one side of that record, full of more buoyant songs.

They'd found the Causeway in a small town north of Burlington, after getting lost during a foliage drive. They parked and walked a wide, beaten dirt trail through the woods and eventually came out upon a long needle threading the vastness of Lake Champlain.

A tumble of old railroad marble littered the sides of the Causeway like some shattered god's tomb. They went out to its break, where during warmer months a ferry carted cyclists and the occasional tourist to the trail's continuation to Grand Isle. The service was done for the year, and she and Ethan stood alone in the center of this great and still world.

Cara remembered the comfort of his fingers laced in hers, a clean wind on her face. Looking across the water as though she could see past everything into the forests of Canada to the north. Ethan had said something about tranquility, or peace, as she pulled her Valium and her Xanax from her shoulder bag. He looked wounded, thinking she'd already tossed it all, but she did so now, spilling the pills from both bottles into the lake.

Her knees weakened and he sank down beside her, pulled her to him and whispered the right things into her hair. "We should make a family," he said in the end. The warmth of the words spread down her neck and she nodded against him, unable to speak.

That day had been the real start of them, three years into their marriage. It was the first time she'd seen a true horizon in front of them, without a decade of chemical haze obscuring it. And she flipped the record over to side two, mid-June, when he climbed on top of her and told her it was time to start trying. But the tumor had already bloomed against his brain, waiting for them to know it.

AND NOW IT was September, its music discordant, and Ethan's evening headaches left her crying in frustration. Why couldn't they have one full day, she asked the next night, giving him his pain pills and a hot wet towel to drape over his forehead.

He told her they would, many of them. His head tipped back onto the recliner, and she couldn't read his face beneath the towel.

She dozed off on the couch and woke to find him leaning over and peering into her face. "Many of them," he whispered. His eyes were wide and gray and shot through with strands of blood. The irises weren't round but seemed a shape she might have learned in school once, of several circles overlaid. As if many eyes studied her.

He left the room when she asked what he was doing and wouldn't answer no matter how much she pleaded with him through the closed office door. She took her last Ambien but lay awake for hours in their bed, pulling patterns out of the textured ceiling. Sleep felt impossible with every moment the one when his voice might come from below.

She nearly jumped from the bed when she heard him. With her cheek against the floorboards, for the first time she noticed a smell under there. Slight at first, but once in her nose it was deep and pervasive.

They'd had a poisoned rat in the wall of their last house. Ethan had ended up hammering a hole behind the fridge to get at it and the kitchen had reeked for days. This was the same unmistakable stink of dead animal.

Ethan's words were so close to discernible. What could Socrates have said that had him so entranced? She could only pull "changing" from the muddle; it was repeated and had a rough emphasis to it. Then came a pause, as if for a small sip of air, and the same rhythm again.

A soft series of thumps startled her and she pictured Ethan having another seizure, his arms and legs rattling against the filthy floor, surrounded by wads of insulation. Thick and muffled grunts, as though he'd swallowed his tongue. She lay on her stomach and could almost see him on his back, staring up at her through the floorboards.

Silence spread out between them as she waited for the sound of him lowering himself back into his office. But the space below remained a blank stillness, and she realized she hadn't heard him climb back down on any of the last several nights. A half-hour later she gave up and crawled back under the covers. He'd asked her to stay out of this. Let him sleep in that narrow coffin if it made him feel better.

She set her alarm for seven and turned out the light even though dawn was already paling the windows. The moment her head touched the pillow she heard the distinctive high groan of the back door opening and closing. His steps passed through the living room and up the creaking stairs.

She rolled away onto her side when he entered the room. The quilt lifted and the naked warmth of him pressed against her back. A scent clung to him, something clean and sharp and the opposite of the stench under the floor. It wasn't until he'd stretched out on his back with a long sigh that she recognized it as pine trees.

How had he gotten outside? His breathing settled, and Cara looked over her shoulder. His lips curved into a smile. His head rolled toward her and he opened his eyes, bloodless and clear and too large.

She turned back and stared at the wall. Eventually daylight strengthened across it, and Ethan began to snore.

CARA WAS OUT of her doctor's leather chair and driving to the pharmacy by nine-thirty, even with no appointment. When she came back home, in the old Valium fog, it was some time before she noticed Ethan wasn't there.

He must have gone to speak with his boss. She hadn't taken him seriously when he mentioned going back to the university part-time. He insisted his headaches were lessening. It was difficult thinking of him in the future tense. Falling into this new routine.

The pills would help.

A couple of fingers of vodka in some juice and the fog deepened. Things were out of place, more than just some critter rotting under the bedroom floor. She knew she had to go downstairs and see for herself, but being swallowed up inside her grandmother's quilt was all she could manage.

She stayed there long enough for time to swell, slipping in and out of sleep, through the evening and Ethan's barked laughter at the TV floating up the staircase and through the parted bedroom door. There were slivers of dreams trying to connect, like torn paper dolls, in which she plunged her hand into Lake Champlain, the pills turning to blue and white stains on her palm.

Sometime in the night Ethan's prayer rose into the room. Cara lay unmoving until she heard his thin moans and the pounding of his fists or feet, then silence. Her fog slowly dissipated into the first clear thoughts of the day. She let her courage slowly build, then got out of bed, her legs unsteady and full of needles as she approached the stairs and gazed down into the heavy dark. Even the house's natural, settling ticks had hushed.

She crept through the living room to his office door. A deep breath and she flipped the light on, saw his cluttered desk, the stepladder upright beneath the closed panel in the ceiling. A book lay on top of his computer, a skinny paperback with a grocery receipt bookmark curling out. It was Plato's *Phaedo*, and an orange highlighted passage greeted her when she opened to the marked pages.

"The seen is the changing," she read just above a whisper, "and the unseen is the unchanging. That may also be supposed. And, further, is not one part of us body, another part soul? To be sure." Just the single recitation carried enough of the near-melody she'd been hearing every night. She scanned above and below the highlighted words, read what the poisoned Socrates had to say on the nature of death as he gazed upon it. She flipped back a few pages. Within many of the same orange streaks was the word *hemlock*. She turned to the first page she'd seen. Printed in the margin in Ethan's careful letters was "Can I bury them?"

A passage of clean text near this caught her eye and she read aloud: "Were we not saying that the soul too is then dragged by the body into the region of the changeable, and wanders and is confused; the world spins round her, and she is like a drunkard, when she touches change?"

She put the book down with a tremor in her hands. A small mortar and pestle sat against the wall at the back of the desk. She'd never used the pitted stone tool, but it had decorated a kitchen shelf for years. Thick white powder clustered in the bottom of its bowl. Half a glass of water stood next to it. She opened the single desk drawer and saw a small plastic bag full of the powder and a handful of short stems with tiny blue-tinted flowers.

Had he killed himself? She knew hemlock was poisonous and paging through the book had certainly confirmed it. She called out his name several times with no answer, each "Ethan" emerging more broken than the last from her mouth. Dread throbbed down at her as she stepped onto the ladder and pushed the wooden panel up and to the left.

The smell clouded against her face. Her heart pounded and the first anticipatory sobs gathered as she took the last step up and stuck her head through the hole between floors. Ethan had left his camping lantern just inside the space. By its light Cara saw her husband lying two feet from her. His eyes were open and blank and his mouth was wet with foam. Another glass sat beside him, empty but for a residue of white paste clinging to one side.

She reached out and touched his neck. There was warmth but it was already fading. She left her fingers against his skin, waiting, her breath—holding a scream or some denial, she didn't know—caught in her chest.

Cara's eyes moved beyond him and saw that the crawlspace was filled with other bodies. It was an interminable minute before she realized every one of them was Ethan. She counted nine, then noticed two more wedged under the angle of the roof to the left. Each lay on his back with a different set of clothes, the lips paper white, the first few flies exploring the skin.

Then she did scream, a breathless keening. Her foot missed a ladder step and she stumbled down to the office floor. She started for the living room then stopped and looked around, shaking her head and saying "No, no, no" in a blind loop. Her pills were upstairs in her purse, an unthinkable journey in the reeling moment. A packet of the ground hemlock caught her eye and she tipped it into the glass of water, stirred it with a finger and then stood there with the rim of the glass pressed against her mouth.

She grasped at her own thoughts. For a moment the world spun around her. It was as though she slept on her feet below Ethan's corpses, watching the hands from her dream lift from cold lake water trailing threads of blue and white, the dissolved pills spilling away from her. A cotton-thick fog peeled slowly back and the Causeway ground to a halt. She saw fierce colors, gold and red across the far horizon.

Her breath fogged the inside of the glass and that too faded. She thought of the X-ray chart hanging from metal clips, the brain tumor collapsing from the size of a baby's fist to a speck of black to possibly just a memory forgotten again each night.

She thought of what might happen if she drank the hemlock. Just the once. Would she be reborn? Would clocks unwind for them together? No pills, no tumors, leaving only a wealth of time. She laid her free hand against her belly and imagined a future beginning there.

A door in the back of the house opened and shut with a groan and a flat crack in the stillness. Footsteps neared—she heard the floor beneath them rather than the feet—and she grabbed the book from the desk. She was stepping up onto the ladder when she felt the doorway fill to her right. A man stood there, watching her, naked and pink. He looked so much like Ethan, but for the first time she knew it wasn't, not quite. It hadn't been Ethan in eleven days, she supposed. It was as if he'd been molded from their wedding photos, the hair a shade darker, the cheeks and jawline as smooth as birth. But the eyes were wrong, millimeters too wide. The angles of his face were out of true in some way. From this distance she couldn't see his old childhood scar beside his ear, the fishhook she knew like her own fingertips, but something told her it was gone.

"I see you had trouble sleeping, love," he said. Cara noticed his bare fingers and wondered if his wedding band was above her, on the hand of his newest husk.

"Who are you?" she said.

"Does it matter?" He grinned and it was almost the grin she knew. "Wouldn't you rather have an Ethan who lives?"

"I want the man I married. I want a family with him."

"That one went and got brain cancer, love." He spread his arms out. "The refinement of him is what you have now. It can be a refinement of *us*. Sifted down to the purest grains."

The glass in Cara's hand clinked against her own wedding ring. She lifted the poison to her mouth again.

"Don't," the man said. There was urgency in his tone but he didn't step forward. "There's nothing it can do for you. Please, think of the baby. Come up to bed."

"The baby?" Cara threw the glass at him. It somersaulted off the floor and splashed chalky white on his hairless legs. He smiled again and something inscrutable waited in his eyes. She reached up and pulled herself into the crawlspace, slid the panel closed.

The smell was how she found him. Dozens of paper air fresheners hung from the back wall and beneath them her Ethan lay bloated in his clothes. His body was the farthest gone. She cleared a spot next to him and stretched out on her back. His fingers were soft lumpy things but she laced hers between them.

Time passed among the remains of her husbands and she heard the weight of the man on the stairs and on their bedroom floorboards. Dust sifted down toward her face. She heard the protest of the mattress and box springs as he climbed onto the bed.

There was life below her and death around her and something not quite either above. She pressed her free hand against her belly, wondered if something bloomed there, and what to call it. Outside was only the world, its great pages of questions. The needle far north in a vast and silent lake like a compass.

For the moment she was tired. The book was still in her hand. She opened it. From her own passage she read aloud and her voice found a rhythm.

ABOUT THE CONTRIBUTORS

KRISTI DEMEESTER writes spooky, pretty things in Atlanta, Georgia. Her work has appeared in *Year's Best Weird Fiction Volume 1*, *Black Static, Shimmer,* and several others. Find her online at www.kristidemeester.com.

GREGORY L. NORRIS grew up on a healthy diet of classic SF television and creature double-features. Norris has written regularly for national magazines and fiction anthologies, both TV and film, and has several novels published under his byline and that of his nom-de-plume, Jo Atkinson. He lives and writes at an old New Englander called Xanadu with his small family and emerald-eyed muse in New Hampshire's North Country. Follow his literary adventures at www.gregorylnorris.blogspot.com.

CHARLES WILKINSON's publications include *The Pain Tree and Other Stories* (London Magazine Editions, 2000). His stories have appeared in *Best Short Stories 1990* (Heinemann), *Best English Short Stories 2* (W.W. Norton, USA), *Unthology* (Unthank Books), *Best British Short Stories 2015* (Salt), *London Magazine, Under the Radar, Prole, Able Muse Review* (USA), *Ninth Letter* (USA) and genre magazines/anthologies such as *Supernatural Tales, Horror Without Victims* (Megazanthus Press), *Rustblind and Silverbright* (Eibonvale Press), *Theaker's Quarterly Fiction, Phantom Drift* (USA), *Bourbon Penn* (USA) and *Shadows & Tall Trees* (Canada). *Ag & Au,* a pamphlet of his poems, has come out from Flarestack and a new short story is forthcoming in *Best Weird Fiction 2015* (Undertow Books, Canada). He lives in Powys, Wales, where he is greatly outnumbered by members of the ovine community.

PATRICIA LILLIE grew up in a haunted house in a small town in Northeast Ohio. Since then, she has published six picture books (not scary), a few short stories (scary), and dozens of fonts. A graduate of Parsons the New School for Design and Seton Hill University's Writing Popular Fiction program, she is an Affiliate member of HWA and a freelance writer and designer addicted to coffee, chocolate, and cake. She also knits and sometimes purls. You can visit her on the web at www.patricialillie.com or follow her on Twitter @patricialillie.

DAVID SURFACE lives in the Hudson River Valley of New York. His stories have been published in *Shadows & Tall Trees, Supernatural Tales, The Tenth Black Book of Horror, Morpheus Tales, The Six-Fingered Hand,* and the new *Darkest Minds* antho-logy from Dark Minds Press. He is co-author, with Julia Rust, of 'The Secret Life of Gods', a series of prose monologues published in part in *The Cortland Review.* David also writes a blog, *Poe's Doorknob* (www.dsurface.wordpress.com), about the many sides of horror in fiction, film, and life. As an arts educator, David teaches writing in public schools, and leads writing programs for U.S. veterans and adults living with drug and alcohol addiction, mental illness, and homelessness. He is thrilled to appear alongside many of his favorite authors in the first volume of *Nightscript.*

DANIEL MILLS is the author of *Revenants* (Chomu Press, 2011) and *The Lord Came at Twilight* (Dark Renaissance Books, 2014). He lives in Vermont.

KIRSTY LOGAN is a professional daydreamer. She is the author of two story collections, *The Rental Heart and Other Fairytales* and *A Portable Shelter,* and a novel, *The Gracekeepers.* She lives with her girlfriend and their rescue dog in Glasgow, where she mostly reads ghost stories, drinks coffee, and dreams of the sea. www.kirstylogan.com / @kirstylogan

KYLE YADLOSKY is a Nashville writer. He's going to plug his Twitter account, now: @KyleYadlosky. He has been published by Scarlet Galleon, Play with Death, and Gothic City Press, along with Dorkly.com.

CLINT SMITH is the author of *Ghouljaw and Other Stories* (Hippo-campus Press, 2014), a collection of fourteen dark tales which, as Publishers Weekly noted, "range from the poignant and un-settling to the viscerally horrific." *When It's Time For Dead Things to Die*, a novella, was released as a chapbook by Dunham's Manor Press (2015). Other stories have appeared in S.T. Joshi's *Weird Fiction Review, Xnoybis*, the *Mythic Indy* anthology, and his tale, "Dirt On Vicky," is slated to appear in *Best New Horror #26* (PS Publishing). Clint lives in the Midwest, along with his wife and two children. Follow him on Twitter @clintsmithtales, or read more at clintsmithfiction.com.

DAMIEN ANGELICA WALTERS' work has appeared or is forthcoming in various anthologies and magazines, including *The Year's Best Dark Fantasy & Horror 2015, Year's Best Weird Fiction: Volume One, Cassilda's Song, The Mammoth Book of Cthulhu: New Lovecraftian Fiction, Nightmare Magazine, Black Static*, and *Apex Magazine*. She was a finalist for a Bram Stoker Award for "The Floating Girls: A Documentary," originally published in *Jamais Vu. Sing Me Your Scars,* a collection of short fiction, was released in 2015 from Apex Publications, and *Paper Tigers*, a novel, is forthcoming in 2016 from Dark House Press. Find her on Twitter @DamienAWalters or on the web at www.damienangelicawalters.com.

ERIC J. GUIGNARD writes dark and speculative fiction from the outskirts of Los Angeles. Read his novella, *Baggage of Eternal Night* (a finalist for the 2014 International Thriller Writers Award), and watch for forthcoming books, including *Chestnut 'Bo* (TBP 2016). As an editor, Eric's also published the anthologies, *Dark Tales of Lost Civilizations* and *After Death...*, the latter of which won the 2013 Bram Stoker Award. Outside the glamorous and jet-setting world of indie fiction, Eric's a technical writer and college professor, and he stumbles home each day to a wife, children, cats, and a terrarium filled with mischievous beetles. Visit Eric at: www.ericjguignard.com, his blog: ericjguignard.blogspot.com, or Twitter: @ericjguignard.

MARC E. FITCH is the author of the horror novel, *Paradise Burns*, and the forthcoming crime novel, *Dirty Water*. He is also the author of the book *Paranormal Nation: Why America Needs Ghosts, UFO's and Bigfoot*. His short fiction has appeared in publications such as *The Big Click, Massacre, Horror Society* and *Thuglit*. He works in the field of mental health and lives in Connecticut with his wife, the author E.M. Fitch, and their four children.

MICHAEL KELLY is the Series Editor for *Year's Best Weird Fiction*. He's been a finalist for the World Fantasy Award, the Shirley Jackson Award, and the British Fantasy Society Award. His fiction has appeared in a number of journals and anthologies, including *Black Static, Best New Horror, Postscripts*, and *Supernatural Tales*. He is the proprietor of Undertow Publications.

BETHANY W. POPE is an American-born writer living in the UK. When she was twelve, her parents sent her away to live in an orphanage in South Carolina during which time she worked as a midwife for cattle. Later, she dropped out of high school to work for a veterinarian. Bethany has performed more than a few illicit surgeries. She earned her MA in Creative Writing from Trinity, St. David's and her PhD from Aberystwyth University. Bethany has won a great many literary awards and has published several collections of poetry: *A Radiance* (Cultured Llama, 2012) *Crown of Thorns*, (Oneiros Books, 2013), *The Gospel of Flies* (Writing Knights Press, 2014), and *Undisturbed Circles* (Lapwing, 2014). Her first novel, *Masque*, shall be published by Seren in 2016.

JOHN CLAUDE SMITH has published 1,100+ music journalism pieces, over 60 short stories, and about 15 poems. He has also had two collections published, *The Dark is Light Enough For Me* and *Autumn in the Abyss*, as well as two limited edition chapbooks, *Dandelions* and *Vox Terrae*. His debut novel, *Riding the Centipede*, was published in June of 2015 and is gathering stellar reviews. He is currently working on a new collection and a stand-alone novella, while he revises another novel…or two. Busy is good. He splits his time between the East Bay of northern California, across from San Francisco, and Rome, Italy, where his heart resides always.

ZDRAVKA EVTIMOVA was born in Bulgaria where she lives and works as a literary translator. Her short stories have appeared in 31 countries in the world, including USA, UK, Canada, China,

Australia, Germany, France, Japan, Italy, etc. The list of her short story collections comprises: *Bitter Sky*, SKREV Press, UK, 2003, *Somebody Else*, MAG Press, USA, 2005, *Miss Daniella*, SKREV Press, UK, 2007, *Pale and Other Postmodern Bulgarian Stories*, Vox Humana, Canada, 2010, *Carts and Other Stories*, Fomite Press, USA, 2012; *Time to Mow and Other Stories*, All Things That Matter Press, USA, 2012, *Impossibly Blue and Other Stories*, Skrev Press, UK, 2013, *Endless July and Other Stories*, Paraxenes Meres, Greece, 2013. Her novel *God of Traitors* was published by Book for a Buck Publishers, USA, 2007. Her novel *Sinfonia Bulgarica* was published by Fomite Books, USA, 2014; by Salento Books, Italy, 2015; by Art and Literature Press, China, 2015; and by Antolog Books, Macedonia, 2015.

JASON A. WYCKOFF was born, educated and resides still in Columbus, Ohio, USA, with his wife and their pets. His first published work was the short story collection, *Black Horse and Other Strange Stories* (Tartarus Press, 2012). He has also contributed to anthologies from Tartarus Press, Sirens Call Publications, and to the revived *Weirdbook*.

RALPH ROBERT MOORE's fiction has been published in a wide variety of literary and genre magazines and anthologies in America, Canada, England, Ireland, India and Australia, including *Black Static*, *Shadows & Tall Trees*, *Midnight Street*, and *Sein und Werden*. His books include the short story collections *Remove the Eyes* and *I Smell Blood*, and the novels *Father Figure*, *As Dead As Me*, and *Ghosters*. His website SENTENCE at www.ralphrobertmoore.com features a broad selection of his stories, essays, diary postings, and more. Moore and his wife Mary live in Dallas, Texas.

CHRISTOPHER BURKE grew up in Cincinnati and spent many subsequent years in Louisville, KY, where he received his M.A. and worked as an audio book editor and bookseller. Christopher's fiction has also appeared on the award-winning NoSleep podcast, and he has contributed nonfiction to www.weirdfictionreview.com. He currently resides in Providence.

MICHAEL WEHUNT makes his home in the lost city of Atlanta. There are an awful lot of trees there, which keeps him happy. His short fiction has appeared or is forthcoming in such publications as *Cemetery Dance, The Dark, Aickman's Heirs, Shock Totem,* and *Shadows & Tall Trees,* among others. His debut collection will see light in 2016. You can visit him at www.michaelwehunt.com.

C.M. MULLER lives in St. Paul, Minnesota with his wife and two sons—and, of course, all those quaint and curious volumes of forgotten lore. He is related to the Norwegian writer Jonas Lie and draws much inspiration from that scrivener of old. His tales have appeared in *Shadows & Tall Trees, Supernatural Tales, Visiak's Mirror, The Yellow Booke,* and *Xnoybis.* He hopes you have enjoyed the twenty tales collected herein.

———◆———

For more information about NIGHTSCRIPT, please visit:

www.chthonicmatter.wordpress.com/nightscript

Made in the USA
Thornton, CO
01/01/24 11:27:48